BOUND

BY

TREASON

BY

ELIZA TILTON

Bound by Treason

Copyright © 2023 by Eliza Tilton

Cover art by Franziska Stern @coverdungeonrabbit
www.coverdungeon.com

Hardcover case character artwork by Olivia Cazacu @ livish.art

www.elizatilton.com

Give feedback on the book at:
elizatilton@gmail.com
Twitter: @elizatilton

First Edition

Printed in the U.S.A

"But behind all your stories is your mother's story, for hers is where yours begins"

—Mitch Albom, *For One More Day*

CHAPTER ONE
MOIRA

Laoise lay in my arms, her body still warm. Blood trickled from her button nose. Tears splashed on my daughter's cheeks, and I pressed my face into her hair, breathing in her sweet scent.

Already, it was fading with the setting sun.

"Your majesty."

"Do not speak to me."

Magic seeped out of my pores, transforming the room into a dark tomb to match my aching spirit. The three priests cowered back as the

•⫶•

luxurious white curtains streaked crimson and the plush carpet hissed with magical vipers. I held my daughter tighter to my chest, unable to make sense of this madness.

Dead?

How?

Why?

"Clear the room," Tallis said, his voice authoritative yet calm. The head of the royal guard forced the priests out along with anyone else who had been lingering by the door.

"Where's the—?" The guttural cry of my husband interrupted my question. His roar echoed through the halls outside, followed by slamming doors.

Tallis kneeled in front of me. "Let them take her."

Through blurred vision, I watched my old friend ignore the horrifying sight I'd created, his sea-blue gaze full of concern. The golden runes around his eyes and nose glowed in the dark, the tattooed mask allowing him to see through my illusions.

"Where's Kane?" I croaked, my mind clearing for a heartbeat.

"Still in his room," Tallis replied, holding my gaze.

I pressed my lips to my daughter's forehead then gently placed her on the ground, remembering her face one last time. Tallis reached for me and I grabbed his hand as he helped me stand. I clutched his forearm for support, tears blurring my vision.

I knew what I needed to do.

And I had to act quickly.

"Let's go," I said.

The darkness shattered, returning the room to the pastel shades Laoise adored.

Tallis nodded and opened the door. The king had disappeared, ranting off in another hallway.

My husband could not stomach the pain, but I would. Grabbing my dress in both hands, I ran down the hall, around the corner, and straight to my son's chambers.

Kane was the last of us. The end of my line and I would not let him die.

Two blade dancers stood outside my son's room, their curved blades at their sides. Tallis nodded at them to let us in.

The door opened and Kane stood in the center of his room, pacing back and forth.

My heart lurched at the sight of him, and I ran inside.

"Mother!" He wrapped his arms around my waist. "What happened? They locked me in here and they won't tell me what's going on."

Holding his head, I rubbed my fingers over his cheeks then pushed back his dark hair. "We must go right now."

"What are you talking about?"

He was too young to understand the politics of ruling, but old enough to know what was happening to his siblings.

"Come." I grabbed his hand, pulling him alongside me.

"Where are we going?"

I tugged him, forcing him out the door and down the wing to the royal courtyard.

"Why aren't you saying anything? What is going on? Is everything okay? Is Father okay?"

Tallis walked behind us, silent, his footsteps a steady comfort. He would not reveal the horror about what transpired this afternoon unless I ordered him to. Nothing would hurt us while the Violent Wind protected us. His innate control over the element of wind made him faster and deadlier than any other guard in the palace.

I placed my hands on the glyph outside the stone arch that led to the stairs leading down to the inner courtyard. The rune on my wrist glowed a vibrant purple, and then the magic shimmered, letting us through the magical barrier.

I had only one option here.

Kane wouldn't like it, but he was not king, not yet, and I was queen, ruler of the surface fae, and it was my duty to protect them and my children from whatever madness had infiltrated our castle.

When his oldest sister, Catriona, died from falling off her horse, we grieved about the terrible accident. Months later, when Sorcha died from a strange illness, we disinfected and purified the castle for weeks, and thanked the All Father no one else showed any signs of the same illness.

But Laoise? Suddenly, dead in her room with nothing but a trickle of blood to determine the cause? No. This was not a coincidental series of horrid events. There was malicious activity happening in the castle and I would not let my last child succumb to it.

Holding Kane's hand, we hurried down the spiral stone staircase and across the moss-covered ground. We passed through the open center court, heading toward the back of the flower garden where a large lilac tree stood. I let go of Kane and quickly glanced at Tallis. He didn't know what I was up to and I was sure he would strongly disagree. My ancestors had lived in this castle for centuries. There had always been a moon fae on the throne, whether as king or queen. It was the way of our people, and it would not end today.

Placing both my hands on the tree, I pressed my forehead against the bark and whispered the ancient words, calling forth the dryad. The wood vibrated, and I stepped back as it shifted and shimmered until the solid bark liquified, and a thin green leg stepped out. A female dryad covered in wildflowers and olive hair that tumbled down her naked form appeared before us.

I grabbed Kane and moved him to her. "Take the prince and do not return him until I call him back."

The dryad nodded.

Kane wrenched out of my grasp, his innocent face twisting in confusion. "I don't want to go with her! Mommy, *please* don't send me away!"

Squatting down, I held Kane's face, his lament staining my hands. Staring into his frightened eyes, I could feel my heart shattering under the weight of the moment. His sister was his best friend. "Your sister is dead."

His eyes widened, the shock making his body go rigid in my arms. She was all he had left of his childhood. He would never know innocence again. I wiped away the falling tears.

"No, she can't be gone." Tears burst from his eyes as his nose began to run. He dove into my arms, the heaviness of his burden saturating me as he sobbed into my bosom.

Squeezing him tightly, his pain amplified my own. He was my little boy, the last of my children. I wanted to hold him there, shield him from the harsh reality, but he wasn't safe in the palace, and even though my husband would reject the decision, it was a mother's job to protect her babies. "You are not safe here. I know you don't understand but there is no time to explain. The dryads will protect you and when it is safe for you to return, I will bring you home."

"Don't make me go," he cried, gripping the front of my dress. "What if something happens to you?"

"I will protect the queen. She will not be harmed while I live," Tallis said, placing a hand on Kane's shoulder.

"I don't want to go. How long must I be away?"

"As long as it takes, but I will send word within a week's time, and I will continue to do so until the threat is gone." I kissed him on the cheek and brushed his dark hair off his face, taking him in one last time.

My boy, who was going through those pre-adolescent years and full of life, did not need to experience all this pain.

"No!" He pulled from the dryad's touch, jumping into my arms, a terrified shudder amplified by his keen wail. "Don't send me away! Don't leave me!"

Prying his soft hands off my neck, I kissed them.

"Go," I said and gently nudged him toward the dryad. The nature spirit took hold of his arm, and he pulled against her.

"Mother, *please*," he sobbed, yanking his body, twisting to free himself and return to me. "I don't want to go away!"

"The dryads will protect you." My voice cracked and I wiped my eyes. "They are the servants of the All Father. It's the only way to keep you safe."

The dryad stepped into the bark, taking Kane with her until both disappeared into the tree. His sob was the last sound I heard.

I collapsed to my knees and screamed. Again and again until my throat was raw and my eyes burned. I fell forward on the ground, digging into the grass and ripping it from the earth. The pain of losing my girls was too intense to take in . . . and now my sweet son, away from my arms when all I wanted to do was hold him against my chest and breathe him in.

My beautiful babies.

Tallis put his hand on my back. I reached out for him, allowing my dearest friend to take hold of me as the sorrow tore through my heart.

"We'll discover what is happening." His thin

golden armor pressed against my back, and I hated that I couldn't feel the warmth of his hug when I needed it.

"I don't understand," I sobbed, curling into myself. "We have guards stationed at night. It makes little sense. There are no wounds. There's no struggle. Why is this happening? Who have we angered?"

Tallis had no answers.

"I must see the king."

"No." Tallis shifted me in his arms until he could look into my eyes. "The king is unhinged and it's better if you let him be."

There were infrequent days when the king was the man I had once loved. More often, he was someone else, finding comfort in his human witches instead of the queen he swore to love forever.

"He'll most likely drink until he passes out." Tallis pulled me out of his grasp. "You should rest. Let me return you to your room. I'll have the blade dancers stand guard outside your door."

"No, I can't sleep. I need answers. My daughter needs a proper burial."

"The priests will take care of it. The king will want to know where Kane is."

"If he finds out what I've done . . . he'll be so angry."

"We will tell him we moved the prince to a safe location and I'm the only one who knows his whereabouts in order to prevent any danger from finding him. The king trusts me."

"As do I," I whispered, placing my hand on his.

"We should go. It's not proper for you to be sobbing in my arms."

I grabbed his face. "Yes. Though I don't know what I would do without you. You're so dear to me."

With his thumb, he wiped my cheek. "I am honored, your majesty."

It was only since I became queen he had to address me as your majesty. Before then we had grown up side by side, best friends, until he followed in his father's footsteps and joined the royal guard. While it should've been my older sister to marry King Axias, I had caught the king's eye and took her place. Tallis and I both had new roles to play within the kingdom and running around the castle chasing one another wasn't one of them.

Tallis stood, holding out his hand and I took it, taking refuge in my friend. "Come on. I'll see if the cook has any food. Are you hungry?"

"No, I just want to be alone."

"Of course."

As soon as we reached the top of the curved stairs, he released me, and I moved to walk in front of him. Putting my hand on the glyph, the door opened. Taking a deep breath, I held my head high and walked to my chambers.

The few servants that wandered the stone halls wept, bowing their heads as we passed. Laoise, my youngest daughter, had been the wild, radiant one. She had filled these corridors with laughter and joy. Now there would be nothing but silence and grief.

We arrived at my quarters, and I hesitated at the door.

"If there's anything you need, your majesty, tell the guards and I'll come." Tallis gave a slight bow before disappearing down the hall.

I stood in my room. A haziness filled my thoughts, and I undid my gown and stepped out of it, not bothering to hang it in the wardrobe. Taking my silk nightdress, I slipped it on and then crawled into bed.

My pixies were nowhere in sight, but it wouldn't be long before they realized I was in my chambers and then the silence would be filled with their cries. I laid on my side, staring out the window. The clouds were low today, creating a blanket of snow surrounding the castle. Warm orange and pink hues cascaded across the clouds, the ending of one life and the beginning of another.

Closing my eyes against the beauty of the sunset, I hoped exhaustion would take me and I'd wake to find today had only been a terrible nightmare.

Something heavy pressed against my back, startling me from sleep. A sharp blade pricked under my chin, right by my neck. I stilled. My illusionary magic would not do me well with a weapon this close to a death point. If I wanted to survive, I needed to stay calm.

Was this a villain who had stolen my children and had now come for me? From this position, I couldn't see who held the weapon. They grabbed my hair and pulled back my neck, pressing the knife into my throat.

CHAPTER TWO
TALLIS

A lone spot of blood dotted the white fur rug in Laoise's room. The only reminder that something wicked happened here. Moving to the door, I inspected the edge, searching for signs of forced entry.

When that proved nothing, I moved the table where Laoise had been having afternoon tea. The last time any of the servants saw her alive. The priests would give me a full report on her death: timing, cause. For now, I needed to sweep the room and search for clues.

Could it have been natural, a sickness like the

last princess or something more insidious?

The queen seemed to think the latter.

What happened to you?

I picked up the half-filled porcelain cup of cold tea and sniffed the contents. Nothing unusual that I could detect. Placing Laoise's cup down, I walked around the table and that's when I noticed a second cup.

The second cup was still full, almost to the brim, as if whoever sat with her didn't partake of their drink. But who?

The door had been locked from the inside when Laoise was found. When the princess didn't answer the call of her handmaiden, protocol called for the guard to unlock it from the outside.

Who had Laoise met with?

A brown satchel lay on the floor right near her bed. Picking up the sack, I opened it and noticed the square sugar chews that Laoise loved. The fruity candy had become a staple in her diet, even when her mother refused to buy her anymore. The king must've snuck the princess another bag. He had a fondness for Laoise, and it was one of his few redeeming qualities.

Leaving the bag of candy on the nightstand, I moved around the room, searching for a break in the wall. Most of the royal rooms contained secret passageways and having grown up in this castle, I knew where they all were. A large tapestry covered the left side of the room. I pushed the thick material aside, running my fingers along the wall, searching for the groove.

My thumb landed on a divot, and I pushed in. The wall groaned and swung open. An unlit lantern hung on the wall just inside the secret corridor.

Making sure the passageway didn't close behind me, I stepped into the shadows. The runes around my eyes glowed, the magical tattoo giving me the ability to see in the dark.

Something crunched under my boot and I stepped aside, kneeling down.

"What's this?"

Shards of glass scattered the ground. A large piece stuck out. Carefully, I picked it up.

The top to a vial?

Did someone poison the princess? If so . . . Moira could be next.

Swirling around, I rushed out of the passageway, closing it behind me and ran to the queen's quarters.

Two blade dancers stood outside the queen's chambers.

"All quiet, sir," one said as I approached.

"Very good." I waited outside the doors, wondering if I should bother the queen. She had been distraught, and I did not want to disturb her if she finally found sleep.

I walked up to the door and lifted my hand to knock before a commotion inside caught my attention.

"Somebody's inside the queen's chambers," I said in a low voice.

The fae standing by unsheathed their swords and flanked me. Taking out my rapier, I motioned for the guard on my left to grab the doorknob and open. When he did, I rushed inside.

King Kyros straddled the queen on the bed, a dagger to her throat, her face covered by her long silvery-blue hair.

"Your highness," I said.

He turned to me; his normal amber eyes were pitch black, barely visible with the incoming moonlight from the open windows. "Leave us."

"What has happened?" I asked.

Grabbing the queen by her hair, he yanked her off the bed. She cried out and clawed at the air, trying to reach him. It took everything in me to not go to her and relieve him of his head.

"Where's my son?" the king growled, pressing the blade against her throat.

I couldn't glance at the queen and risk seeing what she wanted me to say. Instead, I did the only thing I could do.

"The young prince is safe." I sheathed my blade. "He has been moved to a secured location."

"And where is that location?" the king snarled.

There was no way of knowing how Kyros would act if I told him his son was sent to the realm of the dryads and even if I did, I would not betray my queen.

"I swore Tallis to a blood oath, and he's bound to secrecy!"

The king released Moira and lowered the knife to point at her chest. "And why would you do such a thing? You know the magic tied to a blood oath is unbreakable."

She reached out a hand to the king, her eyes pleading. "Something is happening to us. A third daughter gone. Kane is the last of our line. I begged Tallis to take him somewhere safe. He swore a blood oath so that only the two of us would know."

Kyros grabbed the front of her nightgown and lifted her off her feet. "You would do this in secret? I am the king!"

His words ended in a roar, his tan skin rippling with black scales.

I took a step forward, my hand on the hilt of my blade. The queen held out a hand, warning me to stay back.

"I did what I thought was best," she croaked, her face flushing red. "I'm terrified of something happening to him. He is our son."

The king growled and brought her to his face.

"Your grief is making you act reckless. The only blood oaths you should be making are with me."

He tossed her to the bed, disregarding her as if she were a lowly servant and not the epitome of this entire kingdom. "Tell me where Kane is before I kill you for treason."

She landed on her side. "Kane is in the dryad realm, and only I can call him back."

My muscles tensed.

King Kyros leaned over the bed. "I will forgive this insolence because you are not in your right mind, but do not make any more decisions that involve my son without me again."

"Your highness," I said, forcing the king to focus on me. "I will discover the cause of the princess's death and then we can safely return the prince to where he belongs."

The king strolled toward the door, the night breeze whipping his long black hair forward. The darkening shift in color in his normally tan skin gave warning not to anger him further, almost as if the dragon inside wanted to jump out.

"How is it that three of my children have died under your watch?" Kyros narrowed his gaze, his lip curling in disgust. "Maybe I should have killed you when I bit off King Axias' head. Did I make a mistake in keeping you on?"

I bowed my head. "There is no excuse for my inadequacy. Allow me to leave and I will continue my investigation."

The king nodded and left the room. I did not dare look back at the queen, even though I desperately wanted to.

CHAPTER THREE

MOIRA

As soon as the door shut, I ran forward and locked it. With my back against the hardwood, I grabbed at the sides of my hair and a violent sob ripped from my throat. Sliding down the door, I cried, my body shaking, my heart pounding, the pain too massive to conceive. With each cry, my breath hitched and the knot in my stomach intensified. I fell forward between my legs.

What should I do?

Through the haze of tears, I looked around my room, searching for answers that weren't there.

Who was responsible for this madness?

I didn't just want answers. I *needed* them.

Three daughters gone in less than a year.

Kyros had always been kind. It had been three decades since he had saved me from a cruel marriage. We were happy once and then everything changed. Now our past, which was once filled with beautiful memories, would be a grieving darkness I'd never be able to escape from.

I wiped my eyes and stood. There would be time to cry, but not now. If I allowed this weakness to fill my heart and my thoughts, Kane would never be safe.

He could be next.

No, I cannot allow that.

I must think on what I should do.

There must be something.

Heading toward the bath chamber, I ripped at the string of my nightgown, undoing the lace and slipping out of the silky covering.

"Anna!" I yelled, hoping my pixie servant was close by. I had ushered her and her sisters away when we found Laoise. Seeing them sob at my side made it even more unbearable.

"Anna!" I screamed again, this time with more desperation.

"Here, your majesty." She flew in through the open window, her gossamer wings fluttering a trail of golden glitter.

"Help me get this off," I said, looking at the dirt caked around my fingernails.

"Of course."

Her two sisters flew in after her.

The three pixies had been with me as long as I could remember. Anna with her reddish gold curls, Ella with her deep brown eyes and matching hair, and Olivia, whose dark countenance and scowl didn't fit with the other two. Though they were my handmaidens, I saw them as much more, and knew that Laoise's death pained them as much as it did me.

All three followed me into the bathroom. I sat on the quilted bench by the porcelain tub while Olivia turned on the water. Ella, who always wore her hair braided to differentiate herself from her sisters, grabbed a washcloth from the table and dipped it in the nearby basin. She came over to me, taking my hand that was half the size of her entire body. Anna grabbed my other hand and the two furiously scrubbed away the dirt.

I sat, not wanting to think or remember the fear in Laoise's unblinking eyes. Tears rolled down my cheeks. Had Catriona's beloved horse really got spooked and thrown her, breaking her neck? Had Sorcha's true battle been against more than a strange illness the kingdom's priests could not diagnose?

Was this my fault?

A dark curse?

Punishment from the All Father for Kyros killing King Axias and taking the throne and becoming a surrogate father to my girls?

"The water is ready," Olivia said.

Moving in slow motion, the world passing in a haze, my dear friends ushered me into the warm bath. I stepped in, sliding all the way down until my head rested against the cold tub rim, my nose just above the surface. I bent one knee, popping it out of the water. Anna fluttered over and sat on top of it.

She watched me with big, sad blue eyes.

There were no words to express this pain.

"Someone murdered Laoise, and they must be caught," Olivia said, suddenly causing Ella to hiss at her, revealing sharp teeth.

"What do you mean?" I asked. "Why do you think that?"

"Olivia is just being paranoid," Ella said calmly. "There's no proof of anything."

The two pixies glared at one another. I'd known them long enough to understand when they had a secret they did not want to share. "If you know something—"

"Just a feeling," Olivia said. She grabbed one of the brushes and held it as she stood on the nearby vanity table, her short white dress just passing her thighs, eyeing her sisters as if she were annoyed at their silence.

"What if you're right," I said. "I just don't understand why this is happening."

The three pixies went silent.

"It's best not to think on it now, your majesty. You should rest." Olivia flew the brush over and landed behind me, and started running it through my hair.

"I can't rest."

"You will need your strength and mind to be sharp, your majesty. Fatigue will dull your wits and right now you can not permit that," Olivia said. "Let us help you."

I knew what she wanted, and I sat up straight, pulling away from her and turning in the tub so quickly water sloshed out the sides. She squeaked and flew up.

"You can keep your pixie magic," I said, my voice low in warning. "I don't need to be drugged at a time like this. Queens don't succumb to weak solutions."

Olivia's bottom lip trembled, and she threw the brush on the floor before fluttering off into the bedchamber.

"Your majesty, she loved the princess. We all did. This is difficult for all of us." Ella flew over and landed on my arm, her wide eyes filling with tears. "I want to help you. You haven't been sleeping as well since Catriona passed, and now with Laoise gone . . . If something happens to—"

"Nothing is going to happen to me. I'm *fine*." Getting angry, I decided I had enough sitting in a bath. "I'm going to see if Tallis has found anything in Laoise's room."

I stood up and got out of the tub, searching for my silk robe.

"You really should rest." Anna fluttered over with my blue silk robe. I took it and put it on, then slipped into the matching slippers. My long hair wet the back of my robe all the way down to my waist.

A chill traveled through me. "I will rest when I'm dead."

With that, I left the bathroom and unlocked my chamber door. The guards looked at me, their eyes widening at my disheveled appearance before they returned to their position staring forward.

"Where's Tallis?" I asked.

"I believe he went to the princess's room to look it over again," said the guard on my right.

I headed in that direction.

"Your majesty—"

"Don't," I said, swirling around, pointing at him. "One word and I WILL exile you. I am your queen. Let's not forget that."

Anna flew after me until she found a spot on my shoulder. "Is this a good idea?"

"I can't sit in my room. After the king's visit, my head is spinning. I need answers. I need them now."

"I know and if this is really what you want, I'm with you every step of the way."

Stopping, I turned my head to Anna. She slid closer until she pressed up against my cheek, resting her tiny face and hands on me. "Just promise me you'll be safe. I'm scared for you."

Lifting a finger, I traced it along her side. "Have faith, my dear one, and remember the trouble you and I used to cause when we were young. We were a force to be reckoned with then, and we're a force to be reckoned with now.

We will discover the truth."

Guards stood outside of Laoise's room and when I tried to walk in, they blocked me.

"Move aside," I ordered.

"Commander Tallis is conducting his investigation," the fae on the left said.

"I am your queen and you dare to give me orders?" I yelled.

"Let her in." Tallis moved the guard aside. His gaze drifted to my robe then to my face and then back down before he pulled me into the room and slammed the door. "Your majesty, you can't walk around like this."

"This is my home, and I will do as I please."

He narrowed his gaze at me and the golden runes on his face almost seemed to darken with his eyes.

"I'm fine," I said. "I was hoping you discovered something here. Anything that could tell us what happened to Laoise."

"Let's speak in another room." Pressing a hand on my back, he urged me out the door.

Anna hid behind my hair, sliding to the other shoulder, peeking around at Tallis.

"It's better if we speak in here," he said, taking me to one of the drawing rooms. "Let me check it first."

He opened the door and walked in.

Anna had a mischievous smile on her face.

"What's that look for?" I asked.

"Did you notice how red his cheeks got when he saw you? I think you made him blush."

"Shh. Keep your comments to yourself."

Anna raised an eyebrow and Tallis reappeared. "It's safe. Come inside."

"I'm going to go check on Olivia. You really upset her." Anna gave a wave before fluttering off down the hallway, leaving Tallis and me very alone.

I held the robe tighter, realizing that maybe I

had been hasty running out with just this flimsy covering.

"Are you cold?" Tallis asked, guiding me to the chaise close by the fireplace.

"A little."

It would be a few more months until winter would be here, yet its chill seemed to fill this castle now.

"I'll make a fire, sit."

Taking a seat, I tucked my legs under me and rested against the plush fabric. I noticed a speck of dirt embedded under my nail, and I scraped the remnant away. Then I inspected each finger carefully, not knowing what else to do in this moment.

"Hey." Tallis took my hand and squeezed it. "We'll find out what happened. I'm sorry I failed her, and I failed you."

"You didn't fail us. Don't say that."

"Just as King Kyros said, I am the head of your

guard. It is my duty to protect the royal line."

I grabbed his hand within both of mine and squeezed. "Kane is all that matters now. We must protect him at all costs."

"Yes, my queen," Tallis said, his grip and voice a calming balm to the storm in my head.

Shivering, I tugged the robe tighter, breaking away from Tallis. He stood and took the thick fur laying across the settee.

"Lay down," he said softly, and placed the blanket across me.

"I can't sleep," I said as a yawn slipped out. "Did you find anything out? Is it possible someone did this?"

The fire made the runes around his eyes glow. His blond hair that was normally slicked back in a ponytail had come undone, and one strand brushed across his sharp cheekbone. "I did find something."

CHAPTER FOUR
TALLIS

She grabbed my hand and tugged me forward.

We were merely inches from each other, her face painfully close to mine. Her silver eyes piercing right through my soul. "Tell me what you know. Everything. Did you question all the servants? The guards?"

"It's been a long day. We can discuss—"

"Don't you dare," she interrupted. "I need my *friend,* not another advisor."

She held onto my hand, forcing me to speak plainly. "I believe someone was with the princess that afternoon and had come and gone through the secret passageway in her room."

"Who?"

"I don't know, but whoever it was knows the ins and outs of this palace and that is a frightening aspect, but I swear to you once they are discovered I will kill whomever it is, regardless of station."

With that, she sighed and leaned back, releasing my hand. "That shouldn't make me feel better, but it does. Is that wrong?"

Sliding away from her, I sat across from her. "Of course not. It means you'll have someone to blame."

With a nod, she curled into the blanket. "What else did you learn?"

She yawned and rubbed her eyes. The night had drained her and though I knew she didn't want to sleep; it was what she needed. "Rest, my queen."

"Everyone keeps saying that, yet sleep terrifies me . . . what if . . ."

Her voice trailed, tears filling her eyes.

"What can I do?" Staying close, I yearned to reach out and wipe the sadness off her beautiful face. Her ivory skin seemed paler than normal and dark shadows lingered underneath her tired eyes.

"Will you sing for me?"

"It's been a long time since I've sung around anyone."

"Please?"

How could I deny her after all she had been through? "Whatever my queen wishes."

A soft smile crossed her pink lips, and she closed her eyes. I sang in the ancient tongue, a song full of melancholy lyrics, speaking of simpler times, of the grass in the wind, the lilies in the fields, when the fae lived amongst the lands free of walls and rules.

Moira's breaths slowed as sleep finally came, taking her away from this misery, if only for a night.

I could not fathom the despair she felt of losing not one but three daughters. Nothing until this third death had any of the deaths seemed intentional. Her oldest had fallen during a terrible riding accident and the second princess came down with an illness that seemed to fill her lungs and made her cough uncontrollably.

There had been no attacks, not after Kyros had taken the throne. The previous king had been hated by both fae and humans. A cruel fae who waged more war than necessary. His need to control as much land as possible had thrown the fae into countless fights with the humans and the other races of Saol. Even the Magi Council had visited, sending one of their elementals to put a stop to King Axias' reign.

King Axias was not a kind man, and more

than once I had seen the queen crying in her chambers from something the king had done. Moira deserved more and when she found that in Kyros, even though I hated watching them together, I did not hate the happiness it brought her.

The blanket slipped off her shoulders and I tucked it back around her.

Kyros had arrived at court disguised as a jewelry merchant and charmed his way into Moira's heart, giving her the admiration and love her current husband didn't. Until Kyros' real reason for arriving was revealed and he killed King Axias during the summer solstice festival, taking revenge for the death of his brother, and took the crown for himself.

Many nights I replayed that awful day and wondered if I'd had made a mistake by not turning the full force of the guard on the dragon during the attack, even though my queen had ordered me to stand down. It was unheard of to have a dragon on the fae throne, but when the wars stopped, whether out of fear of the dragon or something else, the fae submitted to their new ruler and life continued as it always had.

So what was happening now?

No struggles to suspect that someone or something hunted the royal line, but with this last death, the circumstances could no longer be ignored.

I was searching for a phantom.

Moira curled into herself. I had known the queen all my life and to see her in such disarray unsettled me. Her silverish blue hair stuck to the side of her face, and against my better judgment, I pushed the wet strand off her cold cheek.

If I could reach inside her soul and pluck out the dagger of pain afflicting her, I would relieve her of this burden. She did not deserve this agony.

Holding out my hand, I called my power forth, sending a breeze toward the fire and whipping the hot air back to where she slept. With each soft push of wind, her wet hair dried, and a soft blush crept into her ivory cheeks.

Satisfied she was sufficiently warmed, I walked around the drawing room needing to put distance between the queen and I before I did something foolish.

The lantern on the far wall moved.

Quickly unsheathing my blade, I positioned myself in front of the queen, shielding her from any potential danger. Anna flew out of the hole, and I put my sword away.

Moving to the back of the room where the pixie flew, I eyed her. "What are you doing here? The queen is sleeping."

Anna looked at me then at her majesty, sniffling. "Do you think she's safe?"

"I don't know, and that's why I don't want to

leave her side again."

"That's an impossible promise to make. If the king requests you somewhere else, you must go."

"Then I will leave one of the blade dancers." I leaned against the bookcase, staring at my sleeping queen. "I have yet to hear from the priest who was examining the body I need to know—"

"It was poison," Anna interrupted.

"Are you sure?"

"Did you see her fingers?"

I paused, replaying the day's events in my head. "No, I've been with the queen most of the night. The priests had removed the princess when I returned to the room."

"Her fingers, near the nails, had a darker red color. Olivia said that's a sign of chokecherry poisoning. No one knows poison better than her."

"I found a broken vial in the secret passageway outside the princess's room. Someone had tea with her that afternoon. We need to have all the food and drinks checked for poisons, but have Olivia do it, no one else. The guards are instructed not to let anyone in, but I'll give them the order to allow her inside."

The pixie nodded. "I'll also have her check the passageway."

I moved closer, my thoughts whirring. "What about the previous princess?"

"Sorcha had some type of lung sickness . . . didn't she?"

"Yes, but is there a poison that could cause that?"

"I don't know. If somebody is poisoning the royal line, Kane could be next! We need to get him out of here." Anna's voice rose and I shushed her.

"Quiet, someone could hear us. Kane is safe."

Anna flew closer until she was hovering by my face. "You will protect Moira, won't you?"

"Of course, I will."

"You swear?"

I held out my hand and Anna sat on it. Lifting my thumb, she grabbed it and hugged me tightly.

"I'm scared. Nothing like this has ever happened before. What if we're all in danger?"

Growing up in the castle, I had known the pixies as long as Moira and trusted them as much as the queen. With my finger, I gently stroked Anna's arm. "We will discover the truth. I don't care what it takes."

With a gentle squeeze, she fluttered off my hand. "I'll talk to Olivia, and I'll come back and tell you what I learned."

"Wait," Anna yelped, her wings fluttering faster than normal.

"No," I said. "I fear we need to talk outside of

this castle, maybe when the queen goes to visit her raptors. They're far enough outside and nobody likes those cranky creatures, anyway."

"Fine. I'll have her come tomorrow. If somebody is killing the royal family, we have to stop them."

The queen slept deeply. "I swear to you now, Anna. I will die before she does."

Chapter Five
Moira

Sunlight shone on Tallis who sat across from me, reading a book, the morning light sparkling the runes around his sea-blue eyes and his slender nose. Ever since we were younglings, he loved losing himself in one of the tomes found in the library. I watched his brow narrow as he read, admiring how his nose scrunched just the slightest whenever he came across a passage he didn't like or believe.

"Good morning," he said, without looking up from his page.

He had always sensed me, which made

sneaking up on him when we were younger very difficult. "Morning already?"

Something warm rested against my back. I moved to sit and a soft meow came from behind my back. Laoise's white and orange cat, Ruffles, snuggled against my side. The sight of her fluffy coat made all the memories of yesterday rush back in.

"I think she was lonely." Tallis closed the book and set it next to him. "I can give her to one of the servants."

"No," I said sharply. "Keep her in my chambers."

I lifted the cat into my arms and rubbed under her chin. Ruffles nuzzled against me with big yellow eyes. She was Laoise's most treasured pet and the poor creature would never see her again . . . none of us would.

"I think it's time we return you to your quarters, your majesty."

Even alone, he still referred to me as his queen, regardless of the fact we had been friends since birth. "I told you not to call me that when it's just us."

"And you should know, I would not dishonor you by calling you anything less. Are you ready to go?"

"Yes," I said, sighing, and carrying Ruffles with me.

Tallis opened the door to the drawing room where two guards stood outside. He nodded at them and then stepped behind me as we continued to the royal wing.

"And where's the king?" I asked.

"The king has not been seen since last night."

I stopped. "What do you mean?"

"In his anguish, he shifted and left the castle."

"Nobody thought to follow him?"

"He's a dragon, when he wants to be alone, none dare to oppose, but we are tracking his movements."

It had been almost ten years since Kyros had last transformed. He'd become too accustomed to his human form. I always wondered if he regretted being a dragon and stuck living in this castle. Though he had never complained, never once cursed me for our son. Kyros had no right to be angry with me for anything.

The day he had killed my previous husband and asserted the throne was the day he had an obligation to all the fae on the surface of Saol.

"Tallis," I said, continuing our walk. "Do you think he has gone back home? Most of the dragons are across the sea. There's a few of the tribe, maybe a handful of his own after . . ." I didn't need to finish the statement because it was my previous husband that had slaughtered Kyros' brother. "I just wonder if he's finally had enough of our kind."

"And leave his own son, one who carries the

dragon line? No. I think he needed a quiet that can only be found up there."

We stopped by the large windows overlooking the mountains, staring at the misty sky. The clouds were still low, hovering around the castle. Sometimes up on the mountain, when the atmosphere was thick and dewy, there was a fog that reached from the grass to the tallest spire. That same haze encased us now, hiding Caste Castle from the rest of the world.

No matter how many times I gazed out the windows, seeing the clouded sky always took my breath away. Glancing at Tallis, I thought back to all the times he'd flown me up to the tall spires, using his elemental ability to soar us through the sky.

Things were much simpler back then.

I didn't want to go to my quarters. What was I going to do? Carry on meetings as usual? It would be another few days before we would put

Laoise to rest, and I wouldn't be able to handle mundane matters. My girls . . .

I can't do this.

Why is it so hard to breathe?

Everything in my chest tightened and I stopped, breathing in and out deeply.

"Your majesty." Tallis gently placed a hand on my elbow, nudging me to continue. Of course, I would have to because I was queen and though my heart was shattered, our people still needed to be ruled and if Kyros wasn't here, I'd be forced to deal with our people alone.

Though he may not love me as he once did, how could he fly off as if nothing has happened?

"Are there any couriers here today?" I stroked the cat in my arms, thankful for the soft comfort that seemed to steady my breathing.

"There are two farmers," Tallis replied, falling in step behind me. "Nothing we can't have the chamberlain handle in the king's absence."

"I don't think I can deal with this today."

"Then don't. Close the castle to requests."

"How can we do that without the king here?"

"We will send out a decree stating the royal family is in mourning and no requests will be received until a fortnight. It is not unheard of."

"Yes," I nodded, feeling a slight reprieve. "Yes, that would do just fine. You may go."

Tallis glared at me. "And leave you to walk the halls alone?"

I held the cat in my arms a little tighter. "Am I not safe to do so? Do you think someone will attack the queen in the middle of the day?"

His jaw ticked. He stepped closer, looking down at me. "I will escort you to your room. Once your guards are there. I will do as you ask."

His desire to keep me safe had been something I had never grown tired of. I nodded, thankful to have a friend by my side.

As we turned the corner, Kryos' human mistresses were there walking arm-in-arm, whispering. The dark-haired triplets had been a thorn in my side since the day they arrived one year ago with their cultish ways and strange alchemy. They had clung to the king like a trio of leeches, and he had been enthralled by their hypnotic beauty and seductive nature, leaving my chambers to spend his nights in theirs.

All at once they stopped what they were doing, noticing me in their presence.

The bolder one in the middle, Stephani, lowered her head, her two sisters doing the same. "Your majesty, our condolences. Laoise was very loved."

I didn't have the strength to deal with them. Yes, my relationship with the king had waned before they arrived, but the last time his lips had even touched mine had been after we lost our first daughter, months after the witches arrived at the castle. They came as healers pretending to have potions to slow his dragon sickness when really they came to stick their claws in him and steal his love away from me. We knew little about dragons and this strange disease that seemed to whittle their mind, fragmenting memories and more. The king and I might have had a chance at rekindling what we once had if the witches never arrived.

I gave a slight nod, not wanting to say anymore.

"My queen," the sister on the left side, who had a scar through her left eyebrow, Bianca, spoke. "We know this is a difficult time for the royal family and we are here to offer any services as possible. We've spoken to the priests about officiating the funeral for Laoise."

"You will do no such thing." My voice rose and Ruffles scrambled out of my arms. I marched forward, Tallis a step behind me. "I don't want you or your twisted sisters anywhere near my daughter." I paused, dropping all decorum, finally calling them what they were. "Witches are forbidden on our sacred grounds."

Bianca gasped as if she didn't already know how much I despised her. The only reason the three of them even lived here was because I did not want to stir the king's wrath.

"I think it's best if you leave the castle," I added. "We are mourning."

"The king would not like that," Stephani said, her dark gaze glaring at me.

"The king is not here. And in his stead, I am queen, and you will do what I say."

"You don't have the authority!" Bianca squawked. "King Kyros has made it clear we belong to him."

"That's enough." Tallis stepped around me, gently pressing me behind him. The three sisters shrank back, not wanting to deal with the Violent Wind. The surrounding air moved, lifting their hair as an unnatural breeze filled the corridor, pushing them back. Tallis' power crackled around us, taunting them to disobey. "The Queen has given you a command. You will do as she says. I will have my men escort you to one of the king's private estates in the eastern woods and when the King returns, if he desires your company, we will retrieve you."

Stephani's jaw tightened, but it was the quiet sister on her right, Noelle, who gently grabbed her hand and patted it. "Of course. We will respect the queen's wishes."

I fisted my hands, wanting to throw my magic around them and send them into an inescapable nightmare.

"Return to your quarters," Tallis said. "I will have someone come retrieve you by nightfall to relocate you to the estates."

The three sisters turned and scurried down

the hallway. Only when they were out of sight did Tallis turn around.

A shudder ran through me.

He grabbed my arms. "Steady, my queen."

"I don't want them here anymore. They are a plague among a million other curses that have afflicted this castle." My body continued to shake as the rage inside me begged to be released.

Tallis lowered by my ear. "They will be gone. I will make sure of it. Let us continue to your quarters and know I am right by your side."

It took everything in me not to hug him and thank him for just being there. He stepped aside, falling back behind me a few steps as was customary.

We began our walk.

"I lost the cat," I mumbled.

"I'll find him."

When we arrived at my room, Anna fluttered

outside. "Your majesty. Food is prepared inside."

She glanced over at Tallis and gave him a little smile.

"I give you my leave, your majesty," he said, and before I could say goodbye or thank him, he rushed out and if I wasn't mistaken, he moved faster than normal.

Chapter Six
Tallis

"What do you mean it's gone?"

Olivia fluttered in the air, pouting. "It's not *my* fault. Why are you yelling at me?"

Dragging a hand down my face, I sighed. "I'm not yelling."

"Hmpf." Olivia folded her arms and flew toward the door.

"Not so fast." I snatched her out of the air, and she squeaked. Holding her, I lifted her until we were eye level. "Say it again. This time slower and don't leave anything out. Understood?"

She frowned, but gave me a slight nod.

"Good." I plopped her on top of my shoulder. "Tell me on the way to the death priest."

"I did as you asked, but when I went to the room all the food was gone."

"And the tea?"

"Gone too."

"What did the guards say?"

"You came with a servant and allowed her in."

"I did no such thing." There were many servants in the castle, but usually we had a select group of fae that worked in the royal wing. "Where is this servant now?"

Olivia flew off my shoulder, forcing me to stop. "That's it. We tried. No one is claiming it's them. Everyone has an alibi."

"Someone used magic to get into that room and we need to know why. I want every servant questioned and detained. Whoever has done this will be hanged."

The statement fell out in a rage and Olivia smirked.

"Don't encourage me," I said, taking a breath to control the building rage. "You know I don't mean that."

She shrugged. "If you did, I'd be more than happy to help."

Twirling her dark hair, she smiled wide, revealing sharp teeth.

"Let's just go to the priest. I'd like to get back to the queen as soon as possible."

"Tallis!" An overwrought scream came from behind us.

"What now," I groaned and turned around.

Chamberlain Pelleas panted as he quickly approached. His floppy green hat hung crooked, and his beady black eyes seemed more frantic than usual. "The king has been sighted!"

"Where?"

"On the western shores. He's causing a bit of

ruckus to the nearby foliage."

"Would you rather him eat someone?"

Olivia chuckled and I glared at her to be quiet.

"Don't be ridiculous," Pelleas hissed. "Of course not, but we can not have the king running amok."

I stepped closer, towering over the chamberlain. "Then go and fetch him."

"Well, I . . ." He stumbled over his words and I left him, walking down the stone corridor toward the dungeons.

"I hope Kyros never comes back," Olivia said as she flew beside me.

"Don't speak like that. It's treason."

"Are you going to hang me?"

Eyeing her as we walked, I narrowed my gaze. "Maybe."

It had been nothing but chaos all morning and no matter who I ordered around, everyone seemed frantic and less reliable than usual.

A scream echoed in the lower dungeons, a common sound this far down in the keep. Taking the stairs two at a time, I raced to the lower level and turned right, away from the dungeon and towards the death priest's room. The ancient fae had a knack for dissecting dead things and finding the root cause whether it be sickness or some other odd form.

Pushing open the wooden door, a stringent scent permeated.

Olivia scrunched her nose at the revolting aroma. "I hate the smell of white sage and myrrh."

I too struggled to keep my face neutral to the dreadful stench. I tried to stay out of here as much as I could. Wooden tables lined the right wall and two tables filled the center. One with a white cloth draped over the body.

Was that Laoise's body?

Olivia sat on my shoulder, her tiny hand

resting against my face, a whimper on her lips. Reaching over, I brushed her wings, which were low and pulled behind her back. I didn't need to ask her if she was okay, I knew she wasn't.

"Priest Kolvar?" I didn't see him in this room and had no desire to go into the back room where he kept his experiments.

Candlelight flickered from the open doorway and a moment later the hunched fae shuffled in. His black hood shielded most of his leathery green face, except his eyes which glowed bright yellow.

"Tallis," he said, holding the lantern in his hand. "I assume you want a report on the princess."

My gaze moved to the covered body on the table. "Yes."

"That is not her." He placed the lantern on the empty table. "The princess is already in the purification stage. We started wrapping this morning."

The tension in my shoulders lessened, knowing that sweet Laoise was not laying on that table. "Cause of death?"

"Choking."

"What?" Olivia and I said in unison.

Kolvar tilted his head at us. "Yes. I found a candy lodged in her throat. Very unfortunate."

"That's a lie!" Olivia flew off my shoulder. "The princess was poisoned!"

"Olivia," I hissed.

The priest laughed. "Poisoned? I know your affinity for toxins is unparalleled, but the cause of death was undoubtedly asphyxiation. Pixies, such suspicious nuances."

With a snarl, Olivia dashed forward, but I grabbed her. She bit my hand, but I ignored the attack. "I want the princess to be examined for any poison."

"It cannot be done. Purification has already started."

"That is an order!"

Kolvar shuffled forward. Keeping one hand on Olivia, I placed my other hand on the hilt of my sword.

"You seek blame where none exists," he said. "Do not defile the dead with your accusations. You know our ways and they are sacred. The princess can not pass into the Never without being purified. Do you wish for her to turn into one of those vile darkthings?"

"Of course not," I said through gritted teeth. "But if there was foul play, I need to know."

"There was none. Whatever you thought might have happened did not. Her body showed all signs of choking, vomit blocked by the lodged candy, bluish tint around the lips, a cut on the side of her head where she fell—"

"That's enough," I cut him off, unable to listen anymore. Olivia had stopped trying to fight me and now tears streamed down her face. "Thank you for the report."

Holding Olivia, I left, heading back up into the castle. The pixie cried, her shaking body lying across my hands.

Laoise was not some youngling with no sense. If she had choked on food, she would have run to the door where a guard would have assisted her. Yet, we could not dismiss what the priest said about the other signs.

When I arrived at the queen's chambers, Anna opened the door, her already normally big eyes were wide and frantic. She quickly ushered me inside the room, which was quiet except for Ella who sat at the table sewing a quilt.

No sign of her majesty.

Before I could ask, Anna shook her head and put a finger to her lips, urging me deeper into the room toward the bookcases. She removed one of the books and clicked a lever. The wooden structure swayed open, revealing the queen's secret passageway. Anna pointed into the dimly lit corridor.

"Close it behind me," I ordered, and handed off Olivia to her sister.

The oil lanterns flickered shadows on the wall, providing enough light to follow the secret hallway which led through various areas of the castle. Breathing in the air, I followed the aromatic lily scent of the queen and followed the stone stairs to a lower level. The passageway split going in two directions. Knowing that the mistresses' quarters were to the left, I hurried that way.

A few moments later I spotted the queen pressed against the stone, ruffling her navy dress and looking through an open hole the shape of a rectangular box that was no bigger than the queen's head.

Voices filtered in and I moved beside her, quiet, wondering what she was looking at and why she was here. Leaning over, I peeked through the grated opening. Looking straight into the mistresses' quarters like I suspected. Two of the sisters sat while Noelle, the one I always thought of as level-headed, packed a suitcase.

"How dare she," Stephani said, her arms folded, glaring at an empty suitcase on the floor.

"She is mourning," Noelle replied.

"She thinks we're vile. Wait until she finds out the truth," Bianca giggled. "If she only knew the king like we did, she would be the one cast out."

Moira's body tensed, and I put my hand on the small of her back to calm her.

"Quiet," Stephani hissed.

Bianca frowned and walked to a wardrobe, where she grabbed a handful of dresses. "Well, it's true. She looks at us like we're disgusting and I'm tired of it."

Moving toward Stephani, Bianca's mouth twisted into an evil grin, her gaze widening until all the white around her irises showed. "We should stay. The king needs his medicine, after all. How much longer could it be, until he seeks our remedies."

"We could taunt her into a mistake," Noella whispered, eyeing her sister. "It wouldn't take much for Kyros to plunge the dagger in her heart himself.

"And we can be the victims of her wrathful insanity." Bianca giggled.

The queen trembled and fell back into me. I wrapped an arm around her waist, keeping her on her feet.

Stephani stood. "One more word out of either of you and *I'll* slit your throat. We are close. I won't have your ravings ruin it."

Bianca gasped.

"You worry too much," Noelle whispered.

"Everything is as it should be. However, we have worn out our welcome with the queen. I don't feel safe here anymore. We've done what we can. Let's move on."

"Relax, my sisters," Stephani reached out to Bianca, who took her hand. "The king will return, and all will be well. I promise you. He cannot live without us. We've made sure of that. Without our potions, his dragon sickness will get worse. He needs us more than anyone else, especially his mongrel of a matriarch."

The three started laughing, a creepy, unsettling sound.

Before we were noticed, I dragged the queen away from the cavity in the wall and back toward her chambers. Only when we were far enough where she wouldn't be heard did I release her.

She stumbled on to the steps. Her crown clinked to the ground and she paid no attention to it, letting the jeweled piece fall onto the dusty floor.

"Your majesty!" I held her waist, helping her to sit.

Tears streaked her face, and she shivered. "I'm a fool."

"Don't say that," I said, sitting beside her.

"It's true. Oh, no. How could I have not seen it?" She held her hands to her mouth, sobbing. "Sorcha, Catriona, and Laoise are not his daughters. He owes them nothing. All I had was his promise to love and protect them and I was foolish to believe he would keep it."

Duty would force me to stay my hand, but I refused the order and gathered the queen in my arms. I breathed her in and rubbed her back as she sobbed against me. She grabbed the front of my shirt, her fingers digging into the thin golden chain-mail. I'd let her cry and release the anguish as long as possible.

Moments passed, the queen's cries slowly subduing until they turned into sniffles.

"Your majesty."

She didn't respond.

I said it softer. "Your majesty."

Again, she ignored me, refusing to move from this spot.

"Moira."

At the mention of her name, she pulled back and gazed up at me, her silver eyes red-rimmed from crying. She placed her hands on my cheeks, freezing me solid. "He's a murderer and we must stop him."

"He would not kill his own son. I spoke to the death priest. The princess choked."

"Choked? Have you gone mad? She was not an idiot. Those witches have poisoned the king. A dragon is never meant to live in human form as long as he has. He is a toxin that must be purged from my home." Her breathing hitched as she gripped my face tighter, forcing me closer to her face. She had never been this brazen and her touch sent my thoughts into dangerous territory. "Help me."

"Help you do what?"

"Kill the king."

I grabbed her wrists and gently removed her from my face, the touch too much to bear. "You speak of treason."

"He is not the king of us."

"But he is the king of the fae."

"He has killed my daughters. I will not let him harm me or anybody else I care about." She pressed a hand to her heart, squeezing her eyes shut. "This is all my fault. We should have fought back the day he killed King Axias, but by then I was so sure of his intentions . . . and his love."

I reached over and picked up her crown, blowing off the dust, then gently rested the silver jeweled piece on top of her head. "He swore an oath to you. Dragons are not oath breakers."

"You heard what the witches said. It all makes sense. There's no other explanation."

The lanterns danced shadows around her delicate face. Even in this state, with her face splotched red and her silvery-blue hair messy, she was the most exquisite fae I had ever seen, and she did not deserve to be sobbing on the dirty stone.

Though she was my queen, she had always been my friend first and I could not stomach the pain rippling through her.

Suddenly, she stood, clutching my hand trying to drag me up the stairs.

"Moira, wait!" I had said her name for a second time in a matter of moments. It was becoming too familiar. It had been difficult to switch to calling her by the proper terms when she became our ruler, but I'd worked hard to be respectful and ignore the memories where she was just Moira.

"Your majesty," I corrected myself, causing her to narrow her thin brows. "We must think through this logically."

"I am done with logic and reason. I want vengeance."

CHAPTER SEVEN
MOIRA

Anna appeared in the secret passageway, fluttering in a frenzy. "The king is coming for you."

"What? I thought he was still out?" I said, wiping the dust off my dress then adjusting my crown.

"He's returned and he's not happy," she replied, nudging me forward with her tiny hands.

"Tallis, stay in the passageway and when it's safe, I'll come see you. We'll talk later," I said to him as I followed Anna.

"Do not do anything rash," he whispered before disappearing into the dark.

I quickly slipped out of the passageway and just as I put the book back in its hiding spot, my chamber doors opened. Kyros walked in wearing nothing but a pair of black trousers, his long dark hair slightly tousled and rage in his eyes.

He stomped forward, his bare feet making more noise than they should have as his claws were still retracting from his recent transformation. "Who gave you the authority to close the palace?"

Standing straight, I held my chin high. "You were gone, and I felt it was necessary in order for me to grieve."

"Did you also think it necessary to send the triplets away?"

"Yes, I did."

Anger and heartbreak beat against my chest.

That is his first question upon returning?

"You don't make those decisions. They are my guests."

"You mean your whores."

He slapped me across the face, and I fell back into the bed. Pain radiated through my jaw, sending my anger into an inferno.

If I had enough power, I would kill him right now.

"Do not speak to your king that way." He moved closer and a spike of fear shot through me, but that quickly dissipated once I thought of my daughters.

I knew I should hold my tongue and not say anymore but damn him. How dare he treat me this way.

Holding a hand to my cheek, I grabbed the post of the bed with my other hand and lifted myself up, staring straight into his amber eyes. Squaring back my shoulders, I met Kyros' furious gaze. "A good king would honor the wishes of his queen, especially during a time of mourning. Obviously, you care nothing about Laoise's passing."

He stepped forward, his expression cold and distant, his breath hot like fire. "Who ever said I was a good king? I am a god compared to you insects. We made a deal, and I have played my role."

In a scream, I lunged forward, and he grabbed my throat, his strength forcing me to stay my hand. Instead, I let my magic pour out into the room. The purple and silver hues of my chamber disappeared, replaced with the soft sands and rolling waves of the Aegis Sea. Kyros' face scrunched as the vision disoriented him. The sound of lapping waves echoed around us, the salty air drifting into my nose.

He looked down at the sand squishing between his toes, a wistful expression on his face.

"You made an oath years ago," I said, my body vibrating with power, "that you would be fair, and I would not pay for my husband's crimes. My daughters would not pay for his crimes against your people. We have lived a good life. You wanted to take me to the Aegis Sea, fly me over the waters, and let me experience what it was to be a dragon. Do you remember the promises you made to me?"

Removing his hand from my throat, he slid it to my cheek until I pulled away. Taking my face with his hands, he examined the cheek, turning my head in his rough palm. I could feel the bruise already starting. Kyros brushed his thumb across my cheek, and I flinched at his touch, nothing like the warm one I remembered.

"I have fulfilled my oaths. I desire more and I shall have it. Your kingdom flourishes under my protection. Your precious Moon blood is still in line for succession. All that has changed is who I share my bed with. I have outgrown you like I do these charades of being a humanoid. I am a dragon and I will have what I desire. The sisters are my property and you will remember your place," he said, ignoring the vision and my words. "I will command them to leave you be while you are grieving."

His thumb trailed down my neck to land right between my breasts. "They give me the type of peace you once gave me, until you stopped coming to my chambers."

The accusation shocked me. I stopped seeing him? Another sign his mind was being lost to dragon sickness. If he couldn't remember how our marriage failed, then every oath he made was broken. "That's not what happened to us."

The vision disappeared and I stepped back from him, needing more distance than he was giving me.

His gaze roamed over my body, more

predatory than a husband who desired his wife. The action made me want to pluck out his eyes so he would never look at me again.

"Your memory is as conflicted as your actions. I will honor your wish," he continued. "We will close the castle until after the funeral, but enough of these reckless decisions. I would hate to have to take more drastic measures."

With that, he left and the moment the door shut, my knees shook. I could not believe that he acted as if I was the one that ended our intimacy when he was the one that brought those wicked humans into our bedchamber and between our marriage.

The door to the secret passage opened and a gust of wind rushed into the room. My hair whipped around my face. The table flew back, and I grabbed the post of the bed to keep from being swept off my feet.

Tallis stood before me, his eyes dark, hair

lifting on the sudden breeze and his runes glowing a vibrant gold. The surrounding air moved. I had never seen him so angry. He rushed over as he took my face in his hands and looked at the spot where the king had hit me and without a word, Tallis threw me over his shoulder and headed towards the passage from once he came.

My crown fell to the floor.

"What are you doing?" I hissed.

"I'm getting you out of here."

"Stop." I swatted his back, trying to squirm out of his strong grip.

He slowed his movement toward the bookcases, and I struck him a bit harder. "Tallis, put me down before you get us both killed."

Finally listening, he placed me on my feet, his chest heaving.

"Tallis," I said. His anger was as deafening as his silence.

His jaw tensed; his hands fisted so tightly his tan skin turned white around the knuckles. Tallis was powerful and when he unleashed his elemental ability, he was a tornado. But neither of us were a match for Kyros.

I grabbed Tallis' face, forcing him to acknowledge me. His gaze refused to meet mine. His whole body was tight and ready to spring. "Tallis, *please*, look at me."

When he finally responded, I understood the expression of disgust on his face was not directed at me. The king had never struck me, not once, and that may have been the breaking point for my dear friend. We had to be smart, and I would not let Tallis be slaughtered for my sharp tongue.

"I have an idea," I said, "but it's risky."

If we wanted to kill a dragon, I'd need something to keep him in his human form. Only then would we have a chance. There was only one being who could know of an artifact powerful enough to stop a dragon's transformation and negative their natural magic resistance. Tallis would never agree to go meet the Lich King, but that evil creature was our best hope. A being who used to be fae but then morphed into something else. His kingdom of the twisted consisted of all the devilish creatures of our world: vampyres, zombies, necromancers, and those odd moss-haired lichen creatures.

"If you think it's risky, I don't think it's a good idea at all," Tallis hissed, his expression switching to fear.

That made me smile.

Holding a hand over my mouth, I held the giggling at bay. Here we were in the worst situations. It was so absurd, I had to laugh to keep from breaking. "I have to play nice. I need to think through some things. Make some decisions and prepare."

I looped my arms around his neck standing on my tippy toes, so I was closer to his gaze.

A warm feeling ran through me as Tallis held me. When we were young, I used to fantasize of us marrying, but it was a foolish dream, for royal guards did not marry nobles.

With his gaze firmly on my mouth, he nodded. "Do not speak to anyone. The next time we speak, it must be outside of these walls. If you're in danger or afraid, send Anna to me and I'll get you out of here. The blade dancers will stay stationed outside your door."

"I will," I said, pulling him into a hug, absorbing his muscular frame and how safe it made me feel.

His arms stayed straight at his side until he gently grasped my waist and pulled me off. "Take the day, stay busy. Do not do anything to put yourself in trouble's way. We will figure this out together."

I nodded, unable to form the words, my gratitude overflowing.

He took my hand and raised it to his mouth, where he kissed my knuckles. The touch sent a thrill through me, my emotions bordering between desire and confusion. I wasn't thinking clearly and maybe I did need some rest like everyone had been forcing me to do.

Tallis gazed down at me, the green in his blue eyes sparkling.

"Your majesty," he said in farewell, his voice gruff, then he slipped back into the secret passageway before I could ask him to stay.

CHAPTER EIGHT
TALLIS

The pathway wound through the gardens, past the fae made ponds and gazebos strung with lanterns. Queen Moira and King Kyros walked ahead of me, both holding large flaming candles. My men carried the princess, covered and wrapped in perfumed silk, on a wooden slab, surrounded with heady flowers.

Large braziers lit the garden path out of the palace and deep into the surrounding wood. Caste Castle was unlike any other castle in Saol. The stone keep itself was built on top of two enormous golems able to raise the structure at a moment's notice and cut off entry access by land. The surrounding land full of thick wooded forests and rolling green mountains made the castle both majestic and haunting, especially when the fog rolled in and surrounded the entire keep in a blanket of white. Out here where a fae could overlook the lands, far on top of the mountains, it was easy to forget that we didn't actually live among the clouds.

For centuries, the fae and woodland creatures had cultivated the area into a mystical forest, making it seem impossible that such beauty could live on such a treacherous mountain range.

Throughout the area, the rest of the guard, both seen and unseen, surrounded the grieving royals. Priests and priestesses walked alongside us, humming a low melody, somber and dreadfully beautiful. The full moon watched over the dead princess, its bright light illuminating only her still form.

As we marched to the burial site, I watched the queen. Dressed in a flowing black gown and veil, even dressed in death, she was a vision of beauty. I had not seen the queen in two days. The pixies had kept me informed of the queen's activities, which consisted of visiting the aviary once to see her birds and reading in the court library.

She had not called for me.

In two days, nothing had changed. The king was notified of the death priest's findings and that was the end of the investigation. Though Olivia still insisted it was poisoning, I began to doubt her claims, thinking three deaths of our loved ones had clouded our judgment.

Sage burned around us and the hazy atmosphere added to the somber mood. Sniffles of the servants and the court fae that lived within the castle created a melancholy ambiance. All manner of fae danced toward the hill and valley where we laid our dead to rest. The movements were slow, opposite of the joyous dances our kind were used to. The sending dance was our final farewell, a stomping of feet and hands in both defiance and resignation to the loss.

Near the valley before the land swooped down was an area surrounded by a stone circle. The open dome held a stone slab, an altar to burn the dead. The priests took hold of the wooden bed and placed it on top of the slab, laying the princess to rest for the final time.

Wildflowers arrayed the altar and roses covered the ground, adding a floral scent to the sage permeating the air.

The king and queen walked up as the priests sang, their somber song cutting into the hearts of any who listened. Queen Moira cried and to my surprise, the king rested his hand on her shoulder, pulling her to his side. Had the two reconciled after what transpired in the queen's chambers? Did the queen still believe he killed the princess or had she finally accepted the truth that Laoise choked?

As the song slowed to a stop, the queen held out her flame and lit the kindling, then placed the candle in one of the candelabra holders. The king did the same and then pulled her back as the two watched the fire devour the last princess. Once cremated, her ashes would be collected and put in an urn that would be stored below the castle in the catacombs where all the royal family rested after death.

The queen turned around, pushing away from the king and heading back down the stone path alone, holding her cloak tight. She glanced at me and the pain in those sapphire eyes nearly brought me to my knees.

I could not respond to her, nor reach out and wipe each of those tears off her delicate cheeks.

Stepping out of the way, I let her pass. She was so close and yet more distant than ever.

The king spoke to one of the priests and I decided to follow the queen back to the castle. As we neared the large gazebo closest to the castle, three figures came into view.

The king's human mistresses, the witches.

I picked up my pace to get ahead of Queen Moira, but it was too late.

She had seen them.

Suddenly, the area around us turned crimson. The grass, the path, every inch a darker shade as if the world bled. Lifting a boot off the ground, blood dripped off the side. While my runes allowed me to see the illusion for what it was, the humans were not as fortunate.

The witches huddled together as if they could save each other from the queen's wrath.

"Your majesty," I said, hoping she would hear me and steady her hand. She turned to me, her eyes pitch black and cold.

This is not good.

I had seen the queen's rage more than once, felt the heat from her illusions as she destroyed someone's mind, tearing their brain apart with her elemental ability.

Moon fae were masters of deception and creators of both nightmares and dreams. It was one of the reasons I had these runes specially tattooed on by Lord Demious in Farrow's Gate. As the head of the royal guard, I needed to protect the queen, even from herself.

I glanced behind me to see where the king and other court members were. The funeral was still in procession and no one else had caught up to us yet. Moira's magic had only affected the area we were in and only the people she wanted to see this image could.

The dark-haired triplets moved toward the queen, the one in the middle breaking free and stepping forward. "Your majesty," Stephani said. "We only came to pay our respects."

Like a viper, the queen snapped forward, gripping Stephani's neck with her hand. "How dare you," she said, her voice deep and raspy.

I had to act carefully. With the full moon out, the queen's elemental ability was at maximum power. Even if I could not be impaired by the visions, others could if she lost control.

Snakes slithered along the ground and the witches screamed as the visions came to life, slinking around their legs and crawling up their bodies. The humans frantically stomped and kicked at the creatures, screaming at the deadly apparitions.

I flicked my hand and created a slight ruffle of wind to move around the queen's neck, hoping she would notice me, but her rage would not yield. She threw Stephani to the ground.

The witch snarled, and a dagger appeared in

her hand.

Within seconds, I was over the witch, stepping on her wrist until she cried, and bone snapped. "Leave now while you still have your head."

Someone screamed from behind me, and Bianca lunged for the queen. I unsheathed my sword and turned my body, hand held out as my power funneled within my palm, ready to send the witch flying over the mountains if she dared touch my queen.

Moira side stepped Bianca, twisting her body and stabbing her moon blade into the witch's chest. Bianca gasped.

The queen yanked out her blade and shoved Bianca to the ground, her eyes wide with fury and bloodlust.

The two remaining sisters screamed. The cries morphed into high-pitched wails, the sound like a banshee, causing my head to throb with pain.

And that was when the queen gaped at me, holding her head, crying and shaking. The screeching would call the guards, no matter how far they were, but it was the king I feared would come. If he saw that Moira killed one of the witches, his wrath would be unyielding.

CHAPTER NINE
MOIRA

Tallis grabbed my fallen moon blade and scooped me up into his arms and ran into the castle, moving so quickly I had to shut my eyes for a moment to stop the world from spinning.

I killed her.

I killed one of his mistresses.

What have I done?

No, she deserved it. They all did.

We arrived in the royal wing. The guards had attended the funeral and thankfully none were by my quarters when we returned.

"Stay here," Tallis said, his breath ragged,

once we were inside.

He untangled my arms from around his neck, placing me on the bed. "I'll say it was me."

"They'll tell him I did it." I placed a hand to my heart, attempting to slow the intense pounding. "He'll kill me for it."

Terror coursed through my veins.

"That won't happen." Tallis kneeled in front of me. His voice was steady and sure, but his gaze darted toward the door. We only had minutes and we both knew it.

"How can you be sure?"

He took my hands in his. "It's your word against theirs. An accusation against a royal needs inexplicable proof. Stephani does not want to leave the castle and she knows she can't openly accuse you of murder, especially when all the sisters were afflicted with your illusions."

There was a roar outside and Tallis ran to the window. "He knows."

I looked at my hand, at the blood that wasn't mine.

The animalistic fury sounded all throughout the castle.

Tallis guided me into the bath chamber where he grabbed a towel and began cleaning my hands. He put the cloth into the water and vigorously rubbed my fingers. When the blood was gone, he dumped the dirty water into the tub and pulled the lever to refill the basin.

"You have to go," I said.

"And leave you alone?" He gawked at me. "Not happening."

"You can't be in here," I said, my whole body shivering. Even though I didn't want him to leave.

"There are spots on your dress. The scent will leave a trail." Tallis wiped the wet cloth across my stomach. "Take this off and burn it."

"Get me a dress out of there." I pointed to my

wardrobe.

He went and rifled through my clothes.

After undoing the loop around my neck, I pulled the string of my dress in the back, but since I had requested Olivia to tie my corset extra tight—I wanted to be as uncomfortable as possible so that I could feel something other than sadness—it was difficult to fit my fingers through.

"I can't do this without help," I said, turning my back to Tallis.

His eyes widened and his cheeks flushed red, but he nodded and rushed forward. Quickly, he undid the top knots, his fingers releasing all the tension in my back. "Can you . . . do," he stuttered his words and stepped away. "Can you do the rest?"

I held the front of my dress up as I turned around to face him.

His flustered expression deepened to

something else, his eyes going from wide to nearly slits. The way his heated gaze studied me filled my stomach with a strange flutter, and I gripped the gown tighter with one hand and held out the other. This castle was making us all mad.

"The nightgown," I said.

"Right." He swiped it off the floor and handed it to me. "Do you need any more help?"

Unable to speak, I shook my head.

He turned, moving toward the open window. "He's not there anymore. It looks like they moved the body. I'll need to go down there and explain what happened. I'll say Bianca grabbed one of your blades and stabbed herself, thinking she was hitting a snake from your illusion."

"I hate those witches. Everything started happening when they arrived at the castle," I said, slipping into the emerald green night dress.

I walked over to the window and looked outside at the fire that bloomed in the distance. In all my years of being queen, I'd never made decisions based out of anger or fear, yet since Laoise passed, everything I had learned to be a just ruler unraveled.

My head pounded and I hugged Tallis' waist. He tensed at first, before relaxing and draping an arm around my shoulders.

"We're going to get through this," he murmured. "We will find a way—"

A tremor shook the castle and we swayed on our feet.

"What's happening?" I asked as loud groaning gears drowned out my question and the entire castle moved. "Tallis!"

He gripped me tighter, before leaning over and glancing outside the window, his eyes going wide. "He's raising the keep."

"What?"

Holding on to Tallis so I didn't fall over from the rocking, I looked out the window. Sure enough, the alarm had been raised. The golems, which were a magical defense system, had been activated. Once the king triggered the system, the golems would raise the keep high, making it impossible for anyone to enter or leave on foot. A horn blew, deep and bellowing. It continued to blow as the castle moved higher into the clouds. I felt dizzy and leaned forward.

My breaths coming too quickly.

Everything hurt.

My thoughts were swimming.

Removing myself from Tallis, I gripped the windowsill, breathing in and out. The night air brushed against my hot cheeks.

Tingling started in my hands and crept up my arms. A strange sensation whirled through my head.

"Moira," Tallis whispered, and pulled me

onto his lap.

When did we go to the floor?

"Moira, look at me."

We were so close, our noses almost touching. Cold hands held my face. Sweet breath washed over me.

Bright white lights blinked in and out of my vision like tiny will-o-wisps.

"Moira," he said, louder this time, his voice fuzzy in my ears as if we were underwater.

Gazing into his light eyes, I tried to focus on his face. Blinking back the distortion, I opened my mouth to speak, but nothing came out.

Nausea filled my belly.

With frantic eyes, he spoke, holding me close.

Then everything faded into darkness, and I couldn't hear him anymore.

CHAPTER TEN
TALLIS

I carried Moira to the bed and laid her down. Touching her cheek, her skin warmed and she breathed heavily. This was all too much for her. Pulling back the covers, I tucked my queen in.

This was a disaster.

Standing back, I ran my hands down my face, thinking of a way out of this situation. Though I didn't voice the truth, I knew when the death priest inspected the stab wound, he would see the unique shape, only able to be made with a crescent-shaped weapon. The queen's moon blades were well known throughout the palace.

I need the king to believe the story. It's the only way to get Moira out of this.

My queen lay on her bed, asleep, and though it pained me to leave her, I needed to get ahead of this story. Meet with the king before any accusations were made and discover what the witches told him. If we were lucky, they would not mention the queen. Moira was well loved by the court and convincing them she was a murderer would not be a simple task.

This would work out. It had to.

Her guards had yet to return. I whistled, knowing that one would at least be close by. "Where are those damn pixies when I need them?"

"Are you talking about us again, Tallis?" I swung around to see Anna, Olivia, and Ella fluttering down the hall.

I opened the door and waved them inside.

"What happened?" Anna asked.

I didn't want to get into all the details. Though I trusted Anna, Olivia was fickle, and drank too much and spoke too loudly.

"The queen is emotionally drained. She's inside."

"Tallis," Anna said, flying over to me while the other two landed on the bed. "The king is searching for you. He's furious."

"Stay with the queen. Do not leave her side until I come back. I need to speak with the king."

I walked out and pointed to the guard. "No one but the pixies come in or out of here. Do you understand?"

"Of course, sir."

"Where's the king?"

"He's down in the castle's control room."

"Very well. That's where I'm headed."

I rushed through the royal halls, down the main stairs and deeper into the keep. Guards stood outside the door to the control room and stepped aside as I walked in. Kyros sat in the main chair in front of the window that overlooked the mountains. From here, you could see the stone arms and the sides of the golems that had raised the keep, high off the ground. Birds fluttered by the clouds which were even lower than before. "Your highness," I said, bowing.

"There's a murderer in this castle," the king said, tapping a finger on the control table. "Where were you?"

"I escorted the queen back to her chambers. She was very weak and unsteady on her feet. I think the events have been too overwhelming for her majesty."

He nodded. "I imagine she hasn't slept well. Her grief over the loss of the princesses has made her erratic." He stood and put his hand near the dials. The crystal gears were all imbued with magical runes that enacted the defense system.

"Tell me what has happened," I asked, "for you to sanction the castle's defense system."

"The sisters were attacked outside the ceremony. One was fatal. But thankfully, Stephani chased the assassin inside the castle. With the keep raised, no one can get in or out."

"Did she describe him?"

"No, she lost him in the servant's quarters. She believes it was a fae following the queen's orders." Kyros turned around, folding his arms leaning against the stone control table.

"Why would the queen order someone to do this?" I asked, keeping my expression shocked.

"She's not thinking clearly and believes my mistresses are to blame for Laoise's death, though I do not believe any of that to be true."

"They said this to you?"

"I am no fool, Tallis. The queen has made her

point clear and will use any lie to remove my mistresses from the palace."

I held my tongue, not wanting to speak that I thought the mistresses were also to blame. Claiming the queen had hired an assassin was not as bad as claiming the queen murdered Bianca. Regardless, I had to navigate this conversation carefully.

The king sighed. "If anyone is to blame for the princess's death, it's me."

Before I could ask, he continued. "I had tea with her that afternoon. After my last trip to the Magi Council, I made sure to stop and bring her the sugar squares she loves. I don't need to explain the rest."

My muscles tensed. "Did you eat any?"

He shook his head. "No. I can't stand those awful candies."

"Does the queen know this?"

"No. It will just anger her more and things

are already complicated. For now, I need you to find this assassin. The queen will stay confined to her quarters, for her own safety."

I glanced outside. In all my years, I had only seen the defense system activated once. It was unusual and unlike anything you could imagine. The golems the size of a mountain themselves. The castle built on top of their stony shoulders. "How long will we keep the palace raised?"

Kyros put a hand on my shoulder and opened the door. "Until the murderer is found and killed."

We stepped outside the control room, the king calling the guards to his side. "Where are the mistresses now?"

"In your chambers, as requested."

"Good, come, Tallis. Maybe we will find the answers we seek."

Walking with the king to his quarters, I kept my expression plain and focused. Everything would be determined in a few moments. If I understood anything about the triplets, it was that their greatest desire was to rule beside the king and bear his heirs, though surprisingly none of them had become pregnant.

When we arrived at the king's chambers, the two remaining sisters were huddled on his bed, crying. The moment I closed the door behind us, they ran to him, and he embraced them with open arms.

"My loves," he whispered into each of their heads, making my stomach turn. "It is all right."

"Please, don't leave us alone again," Stephani cried, hanging onto his neck. "We're so scared."

"Shh, there now." King Kyros ushered the females back to the bed.

Stephani eyed me behind his back, the truth an evil lie between us.

What are you playing at, witch?

"Have a drink. It will ease your spirits." The

king undid his coat and tossed it over the nearby settee, then walked to the glass carafe on his table. "Tallis here will ask you a few questions about tonight."

Noelle cried and moved away from the king to sit on the bed, refusing to look my way.

"Of course, my king," Stephani said, clinging to his arm. "Anything to help find the one who slayed my sister."

The king drank, swigging the entire contents of his glass before turning back to Stephani. He kissed her, pulling her against him.

Kyros did not deserve Moira.

Needing to leave this room, I cleared my throat. The king stopped and sat on the settee, pulling Stephani onto his lap.

"Tell Tallis what you know." He tugged at her dress, pulling it down until her shoulder was bare.

While the king fancied himself to her body,

her dark gaze stayed on mine. "We stayed back from the funeral procession. We wanted to respect the queen's wishes. Though she hates us for no reason, we respect her."

"Of course, you do." The king kissed the back of Stephani's neck.

Noelle walked over to him carrying a drink. She lifted it to his lips and after he had finished, he pulled her down to kiss her next. Though it was not uncommon for the king to have mistresses, I did not wish to witness his betrayal.

If I had to stomach this scene any longer, I would not be able to hold my disdain.

Stephani's mouth curved into a smile. "We were about to leave when someone attacked us. Bianca barely had time to scream. He said he came in the queen's name."

"A strong accusation," I said. "Your proof?"

"He had one of her moon blades. Surely, the

queen would not give her precious weapons over easily?"

"If the queen wanted you dead, you would not be standing." A breeze swept through the room as my power started manifesting.

"Tallis," the king's voice warned. "I know the queen is dear to you, but if this is true, she will need to be tried."

I glared at the king. "Someone is framing the queen."

"Framing?" the king said with surprise in his voice. "Interesting."

"Lies!" Stephani said, glaring, hands fisted as she rose from the seat. "The queen has wished us dead since the moment we arrived. She saw the connection we had with the king. She's jealous. The king loves us, and she can't stand it!"

"Easy." The king pulled Stephani back into his lap, her chest heaving. "Tallis has a valid point. The queen would not give over her blades unless she did it herself and well, if you are accusing the queen of murder, we have a very serious situation on our hands, don't we?"

My gaze drifted to Noelle, who could not hide her true emotions like her sister. Her hand shook and she stepped back away from the king, keeping out of his eyesight.

"Stephani." He turned the human around in his lap, gripping her chin, more forcefully than gentle. "Are you accusing the queen of the fae of murder?"

"No, your highness." Stephani's eyes watered. "Of course not. She is grieving and that would be a cruel thing to do, but someone is working for her benefit."

"Hmmm." King Kyros kissed Stephani and began pulling down her dress further.

Only when the king's face was deep in her bosom, did she look over at me and smile.

Taking my leave, I rushed out of the room and headed toward the dungeons. My mind replayed over the conversation with the king. He was the second person in the room that day, but I couldn't shake the feeling that something was off. Why would he not tell Moira? None of it made sense.

By the time I had made it to the death priest, I had more questions than answers.

"Tallis, what are you doing here?"

"You said the princess choked on a candy. Do you still have it?"

"Yes, but why do you ask?"

"Where is it?"

He shuffled into the back room. Dissected body parts filled glass jars along the shelves on the left. To the right the body of a fae lay cut open from the chest, the stomach pinned to the side of the table. The death priest grabbed a jar off the shelf.

"Here," he said, but held on to it.

"I need you to test it for poison."

"Poison?"

"Yes, do it now."

Grumbling, he took the jar over to a table cluttered with beakers and foul smelling liquids. Taking a pair of metal tongs, he took out the sugar square and placed it on a green celadon dish.

My heart raced. I did not want this to be true. The implications . . .

Priest Kolvar took a dropper and dipped it into a clear liquid then squeezed the liquid onto the candy. The square dissolved and a reddish hue spread across the dish.

"What does that mean?" I hovered over the table, gripping the wood to keep myself steady.

The death priest turned his head, his yellow eyes going wide. "The candy is poisoned."

CHAPTER ELEVEN
MOIRA

Something pressed against my back, and I wondered if Ruffles had found her way into my chambers. I rolled over, opened my eyes, and nearly screamed. Kyros laid next to me on his side, shirt off, smiling. The moonlight coming in through the windows landed directly on his face, highlighting the sharp planes of his cheeks and revealing his pitch-black eyes. There was no amber hue in them like normal and his normally smoky aroma had an odd pungent scent. He leaned forward and slid his hand across my hip, a gesture so foreign I flinched.

"You looked ravishing tonight," he said, dragging my body flush against his, oblivious to the fear beating in my chest.

Tonight? During the funeral?

What was he talking about and why was he in my bed? I nodded, not knowing how else to react to this absurdity. The king had been prone to sleepwalking, but never into my bed. Most of the time, one of the guards would follow him and make sure he didn't hurt himself.

Kyros moved quickly, rolling me underneath him, planting his arms on either side of my body. "Do you know how difficult it was to watch you dance in that red flowy gown?" He brought his lips to my neck. "You know red is my favorite color and you wear it so well."

My mind raced with questions, and I thought back to what he could possibly be speaking about. We hadn't danced in a long time and I had worn black to say goodbye to my beloved Laoise.

"Did you enjoy yourself, my queen?" His touch made my body tremble and not from desire.

I didn't know how to respond. I didn't know what he was talking about. "It's been a long night," I finally said.

"The ball was better than I imagined." His mouth trailed up to my ear and I had to bite my lip to stop myself from crying.

Why was he here? What was he doing? What did he mean by . . . the ball?

It suddenly clicked. He was recalling the first ball we had when Laoise had come of courting age. We had brought in all the nobles and spent the entire night, and almost morning, dancing and drinking. I'd worn a thin, ruby silk gown that hugged my torso and twirled with every twist of my hips.

Was Kyros sleep walking? If he was, this was unlike the other episodes. Sometimes he was disorientated, recalling past events, but nothing where he seemed this alert and awake.

"My love," he whispered in my hair. "You're shivering."

"I'm cold. Let us return to your room. I didn't light the fire in here and I know yours is always going."

"Very well." He slipped out of bed and lifted me into his arms. "I will carry you to my chambers and *devour* you."

I gave him a smile, hoping he didn't notice the fear in my eyes.

The ball was before the witches arrived. I didn't know what he was thinking or what was happening to him. Was he asleep? No, he couldn't be asleep, for he walked sure and spoke coherently, but his eyes were as black as obsidian.

He lifted me into his arms, cradling me like he once used to, and climbed off the bed.

Something crushed under his boot and I glanced down to see shards of glass near the foot of my bed.

We left my quarters and he walked toward his own chambers. I kept my arms looped around his neck, watching behind us, desperate for someone to know that something wasn't right.

What happened after I fainted?

When I had woken, the pixies filled me in about the defense system, made me eat then Anna used her pixie dust to put me to sleep—and for once I agreed, desperately needing to forget the events of the day.

Where were the witches now?

What if they were in his chamber and he was bringing me in there?

Going to his room was a terrible idea. I shouldn't have said anything, but I panicked and didn't want him in my bed. We turned the corner, his door only a few feet away. To my surprise, Tallis walked out of the king's chambers.

"Your highness," he said, his brow narrowed.

I shook my head, trying to warn Tallis that Kyros was not in his right mind. He saw my face but didn't react.

"Tallis!" The king placed me on my feet and slapped a hand on Tallis' shoulder. "Are you snooping in my room? You won't find any of those woodland fae we invited in there. Though I know you have a fondness for their tawny features."

Tallis eyed me, and the king laughed.

"I'm sorry, your highness. I was looking for you. Someone said you had called out for aid."

Kyros tilted his head to the side. "Aid? No, I'm fine." Kyros looked at me and rubbed his head, digging his palm into his temple.

"Highness, are you alright?" Tallis asked. "Should I send for the priest?"

"I am sorry, my love," Kyros said, glancing at me with a pained expression. "I'll have to break my promise to you. I find myself with a headache. Tallis, take her back to her quarters."

He patted Tallis on the shoulder before shuffling into his room.

Eyes wide, Tallis quickly walked forward, taking my elbow and ushering me down the hall as swiftly as possible.

"What is wrong with him?" I whispered. "Did you see his eyes?"

Once we were safely in my chambers, Tallis closed the door and locked it behind us.

I grabbed his hand and dragged him over to the window, far away enough where we could not be heard from the hall.

"What were you doing with him?" Tallis asked.

"I woke up and he was in my bed. He hasn't been in my bed in months, not since those witches came. What were you doing in his room?"

"His guards said he was making strange noises and they heard Stephani scream. I went to check, but by the time I had gotten there, he was gone." Tallis took my hands in his hand, gripping them tight. "I found something out."

His voice dropped even lower, and I didn't like the anger in his eyes.

"What is it?"

"The princess was poisoned."

My legs shook and Tallis moved a hand to my waist, keeping me steady. "There's more."

Keeping my breaths even, I nodded for him to continue.

"The king admitted to me he was with Laoise that afternoon and the candy that was poisoned . . . he had given it to her."

Trembling, I leaned against the wall. "He poisoned her then admitted it?"

Tallis placed both hands on my waist, holding me up. "He believes she choked. I went to his room to give him a chance to explain."

"He could've killed you! No, he's utterly mad. We have to go now. I can't trust him. He's a murderer and I'm afraid that soon he will demand me to bring Kane home. I will die before I bring my son to him."

"Give me time to find out where he got the candy from."

"And then what? The Magi Council won't help us. No, I have all the evidence I need. It's my responsibility to save our kingdom." I raced over to my desk and pulled out a little bell, then rang it outside the window. A few minutes later three droopy-eyed pixies flew into the room.

"It's late," Anna said with a yawn as she and her sisters landed on the bed.

"I have to glamor Olivia."

"What do you mean, *glamor* Olivia?" Tallis

hissed behind me.

"I mean exactly what I say. Now make yourself useful and get me traveling clothes." I moved to Olivia, who stretched out on the blanket, eyes blinking open. "Olivia, I'm going to need you to do something for me. I'm going to glamor you to look like me. Tallis and I have to go somewhere."

"How soon will you return?" Olivia sat up, rubbing her eyes.

"Soon," I said.

Tallis came back over holding out a dress and cloak. "I don't understand. How will this work?"

"We've done it before. My magic will hold, but no more than a fortnight." Turning to Tallis, who frowned at me. "Olivia will stay in my quarters. No one will question it. But we have to go now. You can fly us out of here. And as soon as we're far enough away, I can take us to where we need to go."

"Your majesty, I don't agree with this," Tallis grumbled. "We should stay here and continue—"

"Of course you don't, but you'll come along anyway." I snatched the clothes out of his hand and ran into the washroom to quickly change into the cotton dress and hooded cloak.

I then found my boots and I laced them.

Olivia sat on the bed, twirling her dark hair around her finger.

"Are you ready?" I asked.

She nodded and sat straight on the bed. With a snap of her fingers, her body shifted until her and I were the same height. I touched her hand and closed my eyes, grabbing my magic and feeling the tingles through my body. I visualized Olivia as me. The sharp silver eyes, long hair, even the tiny scar on the bottom of my cheek.

When I finished and opened my eyes, I stared back at myself.

"I don't believe it," Tallis said behind me.

"How many times have you done this?"

"You don't want to know."

Anna and Ella fluttered by Olivia, who smiled and walked over to my dresser and picked up my crown. Her favorite part of this exercise was wearing any and all of my accessories.

"Where are we going?" Tallis eyed Olivia, blinking at everything from her height to her skin tone changes.

"It's better if I tell you once we are there. Refuse any visitors," I told Olivia.

"What if the king comes?" she asked.

"Anna, say you put me to sleep because I was frantic with grief." I dragged one of the chairs over to the window. "Even if someone comes in, if Olivia stays bedridden, we'll be fine."

Tallis stood up on the chair next to me. "This is a terrible idea. I still don't know what this *plan* is."

"I know. I'll tell you on the way." I looped my

arms around his neck.

He put one arm around my waist, holding me flush to his body, and then suddenly we were flying. His wind ability moved the surrounding air, a tornado creating a shield and shooting us through the night sky.

There was a pulse of magic as we passed through the barrier surrounding the castle. Only the royals and Tallis could pass through once the keep's defenses were raised. The rune on my hand and the ones around his eyes held a magical marker to allow us passage. Tallis flew higher until we were enveloped by stars. I held on to him, mesmerized by the twinkling constellations. "It's beautiful."

We hovered for a moment, enjoying the splendor.

When Tallis and I were young, I would jump on his back and beg him to take me up past the clouds. Sometimes, he would oblige and show off his wondrous gift, other times he'd plop me on my rump and blow the wind in my hair so hard it would knot.

"Hold on tight," he said, and we rushed across the mountains, leaving the palace in the distance.

When we were farther enough away, he brought us down to the ground. I pushed back my hair, my cheeks hot and windswept. "Why don't we do that anymore?"

"You don't ask."

"Well, you should have offered," I said and gently poked his shoulder.

He folded his arms and eyed me. "Are you going to tell me now what this terrible plan is?"

"Yes," I said, "but you must promise me that you will not get angry."

"The last time you said those words to me, I got walloped by the cook for stealing her blackberries."

How I missed those younger days, when life was simpler, and my biggest worry was getting caught sneaking snacks. "If I remember correctly, you partook of that bounty with me."

"Hmmm." Tallis' face softened, his mouth curving into a smile. "That I did."

The conversation paused and I knew I could not put off our destination anymore. With a steadying breath, I said, "We're going to see the Lich King."

Chapter Twelve
Tallis

"I'm not taking you to the Lich King. How could you even suggest that?" My voice rose, louder than respectable.

"It's the only option we have."

"We should never have left the castle. I'm taking you back right now. There we at least know the devils we deal with."

"Do we really?" she yelled and grabbed my arm. "Listen to me."

"No. The Lich King or any of his minions would kidnap you the moment you set foot in that territory. I'm not risking your life."

"You're wrong."

I shook her off my arm, unable to bear the thought of her request. "You are not some lowly servant. You are the *queen* of the fae and those twisted would love to see your head on a pike."

"Then I'll go by myself. You're being very stubborn."

"Stubborn?" I yelled. "My job is to keep you safe. What do you think will happen if the Lich King's army finds us? They will torture you."

"Listen to me. After Kyros killed King Axias, I had a visitor. A vampyre. One of the courtiers from the twisted. He gave me a message from the Lich King, along with this." She pulled a transporter rod out of her pocket. "The Lich King offered to help me regain the throne in return for a favor."

"You can't trust him. He is pure evil."

"I know, but we don't have the means to stop a dragon."

"Dragons bleed just like us," I said through gritted teeth. "The previous king was able to kill one."

"He had an army of magi. We don't."

"This plan is absurd."

"It's more than that," she said. "The Lich King can give me something that will protect Kane forever . . . He can make him immortal."

"By turning him into one of the twisted?"

"No, something different. A different type of magic. It's called the phylactery stone. I've been reading up on it for years after the Lich King's emissary visited me."

"What does he want in return?"

She turned away from me. The wind blowing her long hair. "He didn't say."

"Moira . . ." I ran my hand across my head, thinking. "This will solve nothing."

"Kyros was in my bed . . . touching me."

Her shoulders shook and I couldn't stay

away from her any longer. Walking behind her, I placed my hands on her sides, wishing I could close the distance, but we had crossed too many lines and I was slipping. Each time I held her, it became harder to let her go. "Did he do anything?"

"No, but he was close." She turned around, gazing up at me, begging me to listen. "I can't bear his hands on my body, not after what he's done."

"Making any kind of bargain with the Lich King is a desperate move."

"I *am* desperate."

It was difficult to refuse her when she looked at me as if I was the only thing in the world keeping her together.

"You are my dearest friend." She placed her hands on my chest. "I trust you completely and I care for you so much. I wouldn't risk your life. We'll be safe. I promise."

I reached over and brushed her hair back behind her ear. "I would gladly risk mine if it meant saving yours."

She leaned into my touch, and I ached to pull her against me and hold her in my arms. Closing her eyes, a tear slid down her cheek and I brushed it away. "Trust me. I know what I'm doing. We will both be safe. I've lost so much. I will not lose you too."

"Hey." Taking her face in my hands, I rubbed her cheeks with my thumbs, gazing into her sorrowful eyes. "Know this, I will never leave you and I will be with you until the bitter end. I do trust you. Not because you are my queen, but because you're my friend."

"Tallis." Her eyes watered, her hands sliding up toward my neck, the air thrumming with static tension, the need to bring her mouth to mine nearly forcing me forward. But I held back, understanding my boundaries.

She looked at me then as if something was different. As if she finally understood the meanings of my words. How every time I was saying 'Yes, your majesty' I'd really meant . . . I love you.

When we were young, I had dreamed of kissing her, even considered trying it, but I knew we would never marry, our positions wouldn't allow it, and I did not possess the strength to taste her essence then walk away.

Her gaze flitted to my mouth and she licked her lips, the gesture sending a rush of warmth through my body. When she stepped forward, I stepped back, knowing the moment we crossed that line there would be no going back. Not for me. I would never be able to let her go.

Why am I even thinking these forbidden thoughts? We need to get moving.

"So, what's the plan, your majesty?" I said, changing the tone a little bit and creating some much-needed distance between us.

"Right," she said, clearing her throat and tearing away from me. "This transporter rod will take us directly to a haven. It's an old, abandoned crone tower where we can wait and then someone will retrieve us and bring us to the Lich King."

"How long?"

"Soon, I hope. The tower is accessible through a door that can only be ported into, but the message was that when we arrived the burst of magic would trigger a notification to the Lich King and they would know we were there."

"Are you sure about this? There are other ways to go about killing a dragon."

"I know, but we don't have time and I will never rest unless I know Kane is protected. If something happens to me . . ."

"Nothing is going to happen to you."

"I killed Bianca in a rage. The witches will

retaliate, and Kyros is unstable. If Kane is immortal, nothing can hurt him."

"What about what Kane wants?"

She didn't answer the question. Instead, she held up the transporter rod. "Are you ready?"

Chapter Thirteen
Moira

"No but lead on, your majesty."

I eyed him, warming at the way he said my name in that soft tone, and then swirled the portal open. A dusty stony chamber awaited us, barely a flicker of moonlight coming in through an open window.

Holding out my hand, Tallis took it, and we stepped through.

I coughed as dust flew up my nose. The musty air made me question my decision to come here. The portal winked out behind us.

Tallis left my side, gripping the hilt of his

sword. He opened the door to our right and we exited, leaving the empty musty room and entering an old lab. Cobwebs hung from the ceiling and covered the beakers. Broken glass coated the floor near a long dusty table. Cloudy jars filled with tiny, disfigured creatures, eyes, and body parts I pretended not to see, packed the shelves. A wooden chair with a cushion, the only seat in the entire room, sat next to an old desk covered in dust. Tallis took the cushion off the seat and slapped it in the air, removing the dirt before putting it back on the chair.

"Sit," he said, and I did. "What now? We just wait?"

"I guess," I replied.

"For how long?"

"Hopefully, not too long."

"I'm going to check the rest of the tower and make sure there are no other visitors in here."

"I'm coming with you." I stood and he eyed me.

"It's better if you sit and stay here, your majesty."

"Your *majesty*," I said, eyeing him. "Prefers not to be alone in a dark tower and would like to stay by her very capable bodyguard."

With that, his mouth curved up to the side. "Very well. Let's go through here."

With him taking the lead, I stepped behind him, grabbing his hand.

The hall had no lanterns or windows to let in the moonlight. Nothing but blackness descended the stone stairs.

"We should probably stay here." I gripped Tallis' warm hand within both of mine.

He turned back, looking at me over his shoulder. The golden runes around his eyes glowed. "It's a good thing I can see in the dark."

"Yes, you're extremely practical." I sighed, remembering the day he had the runes tattooed on and how he enjoyed sneaking up on me, not even my illusions could protrude through those magical tattoos of his.

Taking my hand, he walked down the winding steps to a platform. He tried the door on the left, but it was locked. He continued down until we got to another platform with a door which was slightly ajar.

No light, and almost impossible to see without a lantern. I gripped his hand, quieting my breathing, wondering if we truly were alone in this strange place. It was common knowledge that crones preferred to live alone and because of their odd nature, most citizens of Saol kept their distance.

The door creaked as Tallis pushed it open.

We walked inside and my eyes tried to adjust to the pitch black around us. Tallis' golden runes created a soft glow illuminating his face and part of his upper body. I couldn't see a thing.

Something scurried by my ankle, and I

screamed.

Tallis swung around and I jumped into his arms.

"Moira," he said, using my real name.

I gripped him as if the creature that just brushed me was death itself. "Something touched my leg."

"It's probably a rat," he groaned as I squeezed my arms around his neck. "You can let go now."

"No, thank you. I'm perfectly fine right here."

With another groan, he gripped my waist, not arguing as I held on to him as if we were drowning. "There's nothing in here. It's just an old storage room."

"Can we go back upstairs now? I've managed to go through my entire life without being bitten by rats and I'd like to keep it that way."

"Yes."

It wasn't until we left the room that I finally released my hold. I followed him back up the stairs until we were in the lab that at least had enough moonlight so I could see if there were any creatures scurrying around the floor.

Queen of the fae and it was rodents I couldn't handle.

Tallis walked around picking up random contraptions, looking around the shelves. "There's a chest back here," he said.

I turned around in the chair as he opened the old chest.

"Just blankets," he said.

"Why would a crone need a blanket?" I asked. The crones were a strange race. The stories say they were once witches that had morphed into bird-like creatures due to the high level of elemental magic they consumed. Most magi towers in Saol had a crone. The crone's job was to watch and report on the magic in the land and report any anomalies back to the Magi Council, but this tower must have been in the land of the twisted which the council had forsaken long ago.

The twisted were a race consisting of creatures half-dead, who drank blood, and other despicable things. They were a part of this world, but as the Rift to the Never grew more shadow monsters invaded our world and the twisted had become darker, more insidious. There were more killings around their borders. More humans being turned to vampyres.

I wondered who had been in this tower and why they had left blankets. Tallis handed one of the wool blankets to me and then moved over to the wall that was free of shelves and sat on the ground, leaning against it.

"You should probably get some sleep," he said, resting his head back. His dirty blond hair was undone and covered the right side of his face.

Here? He's got to be kidding me.

I wrapped the blanket around myself, but the

chair was extremely uncomfortable and there was no way I was going to sleep in it. I stood and walked over to Tallis, who rested his head back against the wall, eyes closed.

"Mind if I join you?"

"Not at all," he said, without opening his eyes.

I sat next to him, taking the blanket and draping it across both our legs and then leaned against his shoulder. We rested there and, in the silence, I replayed my daughter's funeral and what I had done. Being queen was not without loss, and I had killed before, but it had always been in defense of someone or something, never out of anger like I did with Bianca. If I had been thinking clearly, I would have used my power to immobilize her.

The ache of losing three of my children cracked me open. The wave came crashing over me, drowning my need to breathe. It was as if the moment I stopped moving, the grief slammed into me, reminding me that my life was forever changed. Tallis lifted his arm and wrapped it around me as I sobbed into his chest. There were no words or condolences said. He leaned his head against mine, holding me as all the emotions flooded in.

Through each sob, I dug into my friend, desperate for comfort.

Sliding down his chest, I rested my head in his lap. With gentle strokes, he brushed my hair with his hand and wiped the tears off the side of my face. Part of me wanted to talk, but each time I attempted to speak, the words never came.

"I'm here," Tallis whispered, leaning over me, his mouth hovering close.

His soft caress eased my sorrow. When the cries stopped, I turned around, shifting in his lap until I was looking up at him.

Worry creased his brow, his sea-blue gaze

watering with emotion. Throughout this entire time, I had never thought about his own grief. I raised a hand to his cheek.

"I'm sorry," I said through labored breaths.

"About what?"

"I've never asked how you are." My voice cracked and I rubbed his cheek. "I wasn't the only one who lost Laoise. You did too."

His jaw clenched and though I could see the strain on his face to keep the emotion at bay, he didn't need to.

"It's okay," I said, brushing his face with my thumb. "You don't always have to be the strong one."

A tear slipped down his cheek, and I brushed it away.

"Seeing you . . . it . . ." I struggled to speak. "It reminds me I'm not alone."

With a deep breath, he pulled me up onto his lap until I was flush against him, his head resting on top of mine. "You're not alone. You never have been and never will be."

Chapter Fourteen
Tallis

The shuffle of feet within the lab instantly woke me. A cloaked shadow stood in the center of the room.

My grip around Moira tightened and she rubbed her eyes awake.

"Your majesty," the hooded figure said with a slight bow, their face completely shrouded in darkness except a set of red eyes. The long black cloak covered the creature and I could only assume it was a vampyre that stood before us.

I slid her off my lap—slightly startled we'd fallen asleep that way—and grabbed her arm, helping her stand, tossing the blanket to the side. "Who are you?"

"Your guide. Only the queen had the rod to this tower. I will bring you to the master."

We followed the hooded figure through an open portal and into a castle.

A throne sat far down the stone walk, draped in a ratty red carpet. Squinting, I strained to see the figure sitting atop the massive black throne, the distance too far to see clearly. Various sized creatures crawled along the sides of the great hall, staying in the shadows, creeping around tables that had long ago stopped serving actual food. Threadbare chairs and curtains decorated the once hospitable palace.

I did not want to take my queen in there. I moved her behind me. Whatever came forward would have to deal with me first. "Do we have your word the queen will not be harmed?"

The guide nodded.

"My guard is not to be hurt, either," she added, and the hooded figure nodded again.

"This is a bad idea," I whispered.

"It's too late to turn back now." Moira shoved me forward a little harder than she should have.

Groans and moans came from the sides as skeletons and the lichen, covered in moss and vines, hovered in the shadows. Red eyes glowed from high in the rafters, spindly appendages dodging in and out of the darkness. Our host sat on the throne, his bony fingers tapping across the obsidian armrest. His green eyes glowed and the spiked crown sat crooked on a balding head with wisps of white hair peeking through. He lifted a finger and motioned for us to come closer.

My muscles tensed. Every instinct I had urged me to take Moira and fly out of this decrepit place.

She walked around me and down the aisle,

holding her shoulders back, hands placed neatly in front of her. Even without her crown and gowns, her aura held a regality only bestowed on royalty.

The twisted on either side of us salivated with hunger as they stalked us with wide eyes. Younger vampyres jumped onto the wooden tables, twitching their heads, their blood-red eyes gazing at her as food. Her brown cloak trailed behind her, and I knew in that moment if the twisted turned on us, I would kill everything in here to get her free.

Holding out my hands, I called the wind to my fingers and created a wall of force on either side of us. The creatures hissed at the magical tornadoes separating them from my queen. Moira continued to walk forward; head held high, the epitome of our kingdom.

Sweat slid down my neck as I focused on stabilizing the wind and raising it until the only thing in the circle of this hurricane was us and the throne.

"Your majesty," The Lich King said, his face sunken and wrinkled, a horrid reflection of the years he had lived. Pointed ears reminded me once he had been fae like us until magic and grim deeds had twisted him into something else. "Does this mean you have taken me up on my offer at last?"

The Lich King was older than us by at least a few centuries, possibly more. He tapped his fingers together, the skin barely hanging on his bones. Unlike his weathered body, his red robe was new and fine golden chains hung around his neck.

"Yes," Moira said. "I have come to accept."

"What do you want from me?"

"You said you could help me rid the palace of the dragon and keep my son safe."

"I thought you two were lovers?"

"We were, but much has changed, and now I require your help in saving my son and protecting the fae."

The Lich King tapped his fingers. "What does the queen offer in return for this assistance? My help comes at a steep price."

"I will remove your exile."

"Moira," I hissed, my magic faltering for a moment from the shock. The nearby vampyres pounced forward and I growled, putting the barrier back up in place and blocking their advance.

She did not turn around and the Lich King slid forward on his throne, his glowing green eyes widening. "And you think this is something I want?"

"Once you were a part of us."

"That spell has been intact for hundreds of years."

"As the queen of the fae, I have the power to

remove it and undo the magic that binds you from our lands."

"You can't do this," I said, and she ignored my pleas.

"But there will be rules," she added.

The Lich King isn't going to follow your rules! What is she thinking?

"Continue," the Lich King said.

"You will be allowed to walk our lands as you once did. Your undead will not."

He leaned back in his chair. "This is what I will give you. I will give you the dagger with the power to stop the king's transformation and breakthrough his magic resistance. It will be up to you to deliver the killing blow. I will also give you the stone you seek. Use the king's blood and some of your son's and put it into the stone and he will be immortal, but once this is done, his soul will be bound to the stone."

"Why am I putting the king's blood on the

stone? Will that not bind him as well?"

"Not if he's dead," the Lich King said. "It will empower the stone. I will give you the words to bind Kane's soul to the phylactery and then the gem must be hidden away. If somebody breaks the phylactery, it will be the end of his immortality. With this, I will accept your offer but my vampyres will be allowed on your land."

"There's no law that binds them away," she replied.

"Yes, but they are shunned in most places, including the palace. I would like to conduct trade, and my vampyres, well, some of them," he said, looking over at the younger ones who had no control over their bloodlust, "make good emissaries. I would like to have one at your court so that we know we have an understanding."

"What if your vampyre decides to feed on my people? I cannot allow that."

"Give him the prisoners. Allow him to feed

on those who are disobedient to you."

Unable to release my hands, I stepped closer until I was almost pressed up against her back. My arms shook from keeping the wind from tearing apart the palace. "You cannot agree to this. We will find another way."

"I am queen," she whispered. "And I will do as I see fit."

"I accept your terms," she said.

The Lich King swirled a finger and a black oval appeared in the air. He pulled a dagger with a jeweled hilt out of the dimensional pocket. The red crystals were brighter than any rubies I'd seen. Using his teleportation abilities, he floated the dagger over to the queen. "This will negate his magic. He cannot transform once you stab him with it."

Out of the same magical hole that stood in the air, the Lich King pulled out a green stone. "This is a phylactery gem. Once you bind your son to it, keep it."

Moira held her hand out as the stone floated through the air and landed on her palm.

"Now come forward and I will tell you the words."

Moira walked to the throne. The Lich King leaned over and whispered in her ear, his glowing eyes watching me. When he was finished, he leaned back, and Moira stepped down.

"Are you able to fix the locator rune on this?" She held out the transporter rod. "It seems to be locked to the tower alone and we need to return to the mountains."

He took the rod, held it to his lips. After saying a few words, he handed it back. "You may use it as you see fit."

"Good." She opened a portal and stepped through back on to the mountain range we first left from.

Watching the Lich King, I walked backward

into the portal, releasing my magic as the portal winked out on the Lich King's laughter.

"What were you thinking?" I said, swirling around at her. Her back faced me, and she held the stone in one hand, the dagger in the other. "How could you do this? Removing the Lich King's exile? I know you're afraid and upset, but you've gone too far. You've put the entire fae and every other race at risk!"

Slipping the items into the pockets of her cloak, she slowly turned to me, tears streaming down her face. "You told me you would be with me, no matter what. You swore to stay by my side until the bitter end."

Seeing the pain on her face, I dropped to one knee, bowing my head in reverence. "You have my loyalty. That is not a question." I glanced up at her as she fought back the sobs. "What we're doing, we cannot take it back, but if this is the road you wish to travel, I am with you."

She lowered herself to the grass. "You don't have to do anymore. It's okay. I can do the rest on my own."

I leaned forward and pressed my forehead to hers. "If you think I'm going to let you do this alone, you don't know me at all."

"I know you," she whispered. She reached up, touching my cheek and then kissed me.

I froze, not wanting to believe it, wanting to refuse the way she felt on my lips. The right thing to do would be to deny her, to stop this from happening, but if I was about to commit treason, then I would go all the way.

CHAPTER FIFTEEN
MOIRA

When Tallis didn't move or kiss me back, I wondered if I had made a mistake. I pulled away, but the moment my lips left his, he grabbed my neck and forced me back.

He opened my mouth, tasting me with the force of the wind. My heart hammered as every emotion for him changed and shifted into something deeper. A connection more powerful than any spoken word. He deepened the kiss, running his hands down my neck, across my face, his tongue caressing mine. At the same time, I wanted him everywhere. I pulled him closer, wanting to feel his chest against mine. I wanted his heartbeat to pound against my own until they were both in sync. If I had questioned his feelings before, I could feel them now.

I fell back on the grass. Tallis settling on top of me, kissing me deeply, my mind ready to forget everything and spend one beautiful night under the stars.

I was unsure of what to do.

This was *Tallis*.

And yet he tasted of everything I ever needed.

When his hands didn't venture anywhere, I grabbed one and brought it to my hip. A sign I wanted him as much as he wanted me. He pulled back, panting, staring into my eyes, asking me a question I had already answered yes to.

Slowly, he slid his hand down my leg until he gripped the edge of the dress and pulled it up. His fingers traveled across my bare thigh, sending an array of tingles that lighted my body. I held his gaze, urging him to go forward, to take me away to somewhere else. Our breaths united, his mouth hovering over mine as he ventured around my body, desire rippling through me as each gentle touch elicited a wave of pleasure.

Our entire lives we had been connected, through the bonds of friendship, through the turmoil of being a young fae at court, and through the simple joy we found being in each other's company.

Now, I wanted to bond with him in a different way, one that would change our lives forever. As we kissed, my magic tingled. His mouth left mine and he gazed in my eyes, our breaths washing over each other. Something changed in the atmosphere, a charge of power and then his magic melted into mine.

It was nothing that could be seen with the naked eye, but the scent of fresh morning air travelled into my lungs, and I gasped. He brought his lips back to mine, kissing me with an urgency that made my thoughts swirl around like a hurricane.

He was my mate.

All these decades of being close to each other, but never truly understanding the depth of our connection.

It's always been him. . .

A sharp pain hit my stomach and I cried out. "Moira!"

He slipped off me and put his hand on my stomach.

I sat up, my heart racing and bent over, crying out as the pain intensified. "Magic." I huffed.

"What's wrong with your magic?"

Digging my nails into his arm, I grunted, "It's Olivia."

His heated expression turned stony. Suddenly, my dress was back to where it should be and I was in Tallis's arms, shooting through the sky. I held on to him tightly as he flew to my open window. He hovered above it until we were sure only the pixies were in the room.

They were crying.

He flew us inside.

There on the bed laid Olivia back in pixie form, bleeding from her stomach.

"Moira!" Anna cried, and I ran to her side, the pain in my stomach gone.

"What happened?" My hands shook as I reached for Olivia and gently placed a finger on her forehead. She was burning up.

"The king came in here asking you a bunch of strange questions." Anna flew over to a pail of water and took out a wet rag then brought it over to Olivia to gently lay it across the pixie's hot head. "Everything went chaotic then ... he wasn't himself. He accused you of killing Bianca and then . . ."

Tallis said eyed me with a worried expression.

If the witches told him the truth, I wasn't safe. "Stay here. Don't leave. Where's the king now?"

"Storming through the castle," Anna said. "He saw Olivia transform. He's looking for you, Moira. If he finds you, I don't know what he'll do."

"I'll be fine. Tallis, find him. I will stay here and do everything I can to help Olivia."

He nodded and flew out the window.

I looked at Olivia who bled out on my blankets. "I'm sorry. I'm so sorry."

She cried and grabbed hold of my hand. Her sisters flew closer. "We can take her somewhere. Maybe the priestesses can help."

"There's too much blood," Ella said and placed a brown salve on the wound that made Olivia scream. "I'll try and do everything I can to stop the bleeding."

"This was my fault. I should never have made Olivia pretend to be me." I was losing a part of myself. Another person I cared for in danger of dying right before my eyes. I bent over and kissed the top of Olivia's head.

Ella sprinkled silver dust across Olivia's body, whispering. The magical powder sunk into Olivia's body and her face relaxed. "That should help ease the pain."

I need to end this.

He will not hurt anyone else.

"Stay here." I went to my dresser and grabbed my moon blade and shoved it into my cloak.

"Where are you going?" Anna flew to the bookcase, a meager attempt to block me.

"I'm going to the king's chambers and when he arrives, I'll be ready for him." Before Anna could argue, I slipped around her and into the secret passageway.

I refused to let anyone else I cared about die. He killed my daughters and stabbed my friend. If he thought he was stabbing me then I needed to act quickly.

Rage filled my thoughts, washing away any fear. I didn't care what the consequences were. I was queen of the fae and my job was to protect them and my family. This wasn't treason. This was duty. He wasn't our king. He was a usurper I stupidly fell for.

I followed the corridor to the left, which curved toward the king's quarters. I waited, looking through the peephole to see if he was in the room. When I heard nothing, I pressed down on the latch and the wall opened. I stepped into the quiet bedroom bathed in firelight from the fireplace. I thought of where I should stand. If I should stay by the door and attack him when he first walked in or something else.

I examined his bed, looking at the messy covers. Remembering that once we were lovers. But that time had long passed, and I did not miss it. I touched my lips, still tasting Tallis on them and wondering if we would ever have a chance to be together. If we both survived, then what? I was queen. I couldn't marry him, and yet I could never be with anyone else.

The drawer to the nightstand was open and I peeked inside. There were some coins, cigars, and a black velvet case. I opened the case and saw six clear vials, one empty. I took one and undid the top and smelled it. There was a distinct scent of mushroom, valerian, and something else I couldn't place. A floral aroma, but what was this? It wasn't a tonic I knew of. He had suffered from insomnia, and it wasn't uncommon for him to take a sleeping potion, but this was something else.

This was some type of psychedelic, something to cause illusions.

Why would Kyros have such a thing? Was this the medication the witches had been giving him? They were supposed to be slowing the dragon sickness, not making it worse.

The door opened and I spun around, holding the vial. Kyros glared at me, splattered blood on his white shirt as if he was the one who had been stabbed.

"What is this?" I held up the empty vial.

He stomped forward, taking the bottle out of my hand and the box and shoving both back in the drawer. "Where were you? Why would you glamor your pixie?"

"Why did you kill her? Were you trying to kill me?"

"She's a pixie," he said with utter disgust. "I'm surprised she's lived this long. Replace her if you wish and no, I saw through your weak glamor. The illusion was fading."

I stepped back in horror. "Replace her? Olivia has been my friend and my attendant since I was young. Have you no heart? What has happened to you? You once cared about all the things I did."

"You know what I care about?" he said, holding his finger out and poking me in the chest. "I care about my son. Your grief has taken over any sense. I've been patient with you, but that leniency ends now."

At the mention of Kane, I stilled, remembering my purpose here.

"It's time to end this madness."

"No. You've gone completely mad."

"I'm mad?" His voice rose. "You call me mad after what you have done?"

"Me?"

He pushed forward. The back of my legs hit the bed.

"I've heard of how you speak about me. The whispers, the rumors. How many times have you wished me dead? And I'm beginning to think there was no assassin and you were the one to kill Bianca. Whether out of jealousy or pure insanity."

"Is that what your whores are telling you?" I yelled, sliding away from him. "The witches that whisper cruel deeds in your ear."

"You will bring my son back home."

"Never."

He screamed and I dashed around the bed. He snatched my cloak and dragged me closer until he could grab my hair. "You will do as I say or I will burn this entire palace to the ground and you along with it."

Yanking my head back, I elbowed him in the stomach. With a roar, he slammed me into the bed, releasing my hair. I rolled across the mattress, calling my magic around me. A magical viper snapped at his face. He stumbled back, swatting the vision, and it gave me enough time to crawl out from under him.

Sliding my hand into the pocket of my cloak, I gripped the dagger hilt.

Kyros leaped onto the bed, grabbing my throat and pressing me back into the pillow. "You will not take him from me."

Casting a shimmer around my body to distort the surrounding air, I slid out the dagger.

"You will never see your son again."

I stabbed the blade into his stomach, twisting the weapon as I drove it in deeper.

Kyros stumbled back, pulling the dagger out of his stomach and dropping it to the floor, his expression shocked. Pressing a hand onto the gushing wound, he gazed at me with disbelief and then rage.

My heartbeat roared in my ear.

Kill him now.

Do it quickly!

He yelled, and then his eyes widened with fear. Glancing at the blood running down his stomach to his leg, he bellowed again and yet his body did not transform. "Why can't I transform? What is this? Dark Magic? They were right about you."

He backed away. I scrambled off the bed.

"You're the witch," he whispered, looking at me in horror. "The one haunting my dreams. You were the one they've warned me about. My death bringer was always you..."

"I don't know what you're talking about," I said, glancing around the room. I needed to end it now. Would that wound kill him? No, the Lich King said it would only negate his transformation.

Just then the bedroom door opened.

Stephani lunged for me. I quickly pulled out my moonblade and slashed, but she dodged the blow and punched me in the face, sending me flying backwards.

White spots speckled my vision as pain radiated out from my cheek.

"Traitor!" she screamed, scrambling over me,

grabbing my hair and landing on my back. "You attacked the king. You will be hanged for this."

"He killed my daughters. He deserves more than death." I rolled over and spit in her face.

She shrieked and clawed at my clothes, trying to reach me as I rushed toward the door. I twisted at the last minute, angling the moonblade, ready to end her life. She vaulted forward, grabbing my arm that held the weapon and bit into my wrist.

I screamed as searing pain ripped through my arm and I fell to the ground, dropping my weapon. Stephanie spat a wad of blood out of her mouth and snatched up my moonblade and rose it over her head.

"I've been waiting for this moment," she snarled.

I held out my hands, lurching away from her on the ground.

"With the queen out of the way, the king will

need a new queen, new heirs, ones better suited to overseeing your unruly kind. The age of the dragonborn will return." She launched for me.

I rolled to the side and the blade hit my shoulder. I cried as it pierced flesh. Calling my power forth, dark shadows swirled around Stephani, enclosing her in darkness and I kicked her in the chest, shoving her off.

"Your time has come," she said, swatting wildly. "My plans are finally fulfilled."

"Has that always been your plan?" I asked through gritted teeth, crawling across the floor, holding my shoulder. "To get rid of me and my daughters so you can sit on the throne?"

Stephani laughed. "The world *is* a better place with them gone, isn't it? And now that you will be gone, the king and I will have our happily ever after."

Quickly, getting to my feet, I dashed away from her. She spun and jumped, launching herself in my direction. White spots speckled my vision and I swayed, losing my footing and the vision broke.

Her dark eyes widened with a wicked glee as she emerged from the dissipating cloud. With the moonblade aiming for me, I held up my hands to block the incoming blow and something stepped between us.

Kyros.

The curved blade embedded directly into his heart.

"No! What are you doing?" Stephanie stepped back, horror on her face.

"What was your plan?" He slid the moonblade out, tossing it aside.

"My love. I wanted us to be together. To rule like we dreamed about."

"Who killed the princesses?"

"Kyros," she said, reaching out to place a hand on his chest.

"You will address me as king!" He leaned into the dresser, and she stared at him.

"You need a priest," she said. "I'll go get one."

"You will stay and answer my questions. Who committed these atrocities?"

With a quizzical look, she tilted her head at him. "My love, you did."

"What? I didn't kill the princesses."

"Not that you remember, but it was you nonetheless."

He stumbled as if the news hit him in a way he wasn't ready to remember. "I have never harmed those girls."

Stephani's face shifted, a cruel gleam in her eyes and she grabbed his arm. "It's such a shame you had those awful lucid dreams. Dragon sickness is such a terrible disease and one you suffer because the fae don't understand the needs of a dragon. I do though."

He shoved her off as he slid into the dresser,

slipping to the floor.

"And poor Laoise. I'm sure she suffered terribly from those candies you gave her."

"It was you?" I glared at the witch. "And what if the king had eaten your poisoned candy?"

"We're not fools like you fae," she smirked. "We had plenty of antidotes already in his tonics."

Kyros gazed over at me, confused. "I would never hurt them. Not just because I promised you, but because I loved them."

Tears streamed down my face. There was no lie in his amber eyes. I covered his wound with my hands. Blood gushed around my fingers.

He glared at the witch. "The princesses were my daughters, even if not by blood. I would never have harmed them."

"No, and yet when you went riding with Catriona and she fell, you did nothing. When Sorcha fell ill it was you who gave her that medicine to help heal her which only made it worse—that one I tried to warn you, but your mind does not remember events clearly."

With a growl, Kyros moved, and I pressed him back. "Don't. You're losing too much blood."

Stephani laughed. "I'm going to find a priest before he dies, and all of this was pointless."

She turned around and walked right into Tallis' sword. He shoved the blade through her chest and then yanked it back out. She looked at him in shock before slumping to the floor.

Tallis' gaze flew to me then to the king before he ran to us. "I'll get help."

"No," Kyros croaked and grabbed Tallis' arm. "Whatever Moira stabbed me with, it's not just my ability to transform . . . but to heal. The wound is too deep."

"I overheard them say that it was you. Then the other night when you came to me as if it was the night of the ball. I thought you had gone

mad. I thought you killed them and after Olivia
. . . I didn't . . ."

He leaned his head against the wall.

A guard ran in. He gawked at the dead body on
the floor then to Tallis, who still held the bloody
sword. The guard's eyes widened at the king
bleeding out against the dresser. "The King has
been attacked!" He immediately unsheathed
his weapon.

"No," Tallis said, trying to stop the guard
from advancing. He parried the attack and
pushed the guard back. "Get help," he ordered.

The guard snarled. "You will pay for this,
Tallis. We've all seen how you look at the queen.
It appears you've finally made your move."

The guard dashed from the room, yelling for
aid as he ran.

"Go now," Kyros groaned. "I will explain it
was Stephani. Bring me Kane. I want to see him
before I die."

Tallis grabbed my hand, but I pulled away staring at Kyros. "I'm sorry."

"Our relationship began with a lie," Kyros whispered. "It is only right that it ends on one."

CHAPTER SIXTEEN
TALLIS

"Take her," the king ordered, "and keep her safe."

I pulled Moira into the secret passageway, running through the dark corridor. We had played in these halls our entire lives and I knew that we would have to go to her room if we wanted to get to the royal courtyard quicker, but in that room, lay our friend bleeding out. Instead, I took Moira deeper into the keep through the servants' quarters.

"This way," I said, keeping her close.

Some of the guards teased me about Moira.

No matter how hard I tried to keep my feelings out of my expressions, there were moments when the queen would speak and admiration would flow through my gaze.

She held on to my side, racing through the secret passageway.

When we reached the bottom stairwell, I opened the door and peeked out. Surprisingly, there was nobody in this area and I pulled her out and ran toward the side entrance. Once I reached one of the doors, I looped my arm around her waist and flew her up into the sky.

Blood covered the front of her dress and dripped down her wrist. Splashes of it smeared her pale face. I held her tight as we ascended high above the castle. The royal courtyard was open to the elements though a wall had been raised out of the ground to keep it enclosed and tied to the castle.

Slowly, we descended to the mossy floor near

the giant tree where we had last seen her son. The barrier tingled as we passed through and then I gently placed Moira on the ground.

She breathed heavily. Her silvery blue hair was streaked with blood and when she brushed her hair back, she dragged a smear of red through it. Silver eyes stained with tears and a worried expression painted her face. She pushed past me to the tree and put her hands on top of it. Touching the bark, she whispered in the ancient tongue, knowing that somewhere deep within the dryad realm, her plea would be heard.

I gathered her in my arms, allowing her to lean against my chest. "What happened? I heard Stephani at the end talking about the princesses."

"She tried to kill me and Kyros blocked the attack. It was the witches . . . they were behind it all. I should have killed them the moment they arrived at the castle then none of this would have happened."

We stood back, as a warm glow emitted from the tree. I released Moira, not wanting to add any more questions to the already dire situation. A tall fae walked out, pale skin like Moira, but with dark hair down to his waist. He wore black pants and a black shirt. His piercing silver eyes seemed to seethe with power.

"Who are you?" I asked, already moving closer.

"I suppose you would forget about me after forty years."

Moira's eyes widened and walked forward. "It can't be. It's not even been a week."

He folded his arms. "For you, maybe, but for me it's been much longer."

Impossible.

This was Kane?

But I knew little about the strange realm.

Moira had disappeared once when we were young, just for a few hours. When she returned, saying she had gone to live with the trees, she hadn't aged at all.

"You left me alone for decades in a strange world. Without any answers, not once did you come to check on me."

"Kane. I—"

"I don't care to hear your excuses, mother." His mouth twisted in a snarl, so similar to his father. "Why is there blood on your hands? What has happened?"

Moira stood there in shock, and I knew I needed to handle this conversation. "The king has been attacked. You need to go to your father's chambers. Right now. He doesn't have much time left."

Without a word, Kane glared at Moira then raced toward the raised wall. He jumped up, black claws protruding from his fingers, and latched into the stone, climbing toward the castle.

"My boy." Moira fell to her knees, grasping at the earth. "This can't be happening."

A horn blew, long and loud. The deep, bellowing sound could only mean one thing.

The king was dead.

Moira looked up at me and it broke my heart to see the utter hopelessness and confusion in her eyes.

"Steady, my queen." I lifted her into my arms and flew up, taking her back to her chambers where Anna and Ella sat on the bed next to a sleeping Olivia. The wound seemed to be closed enough to stop the bleeding.

Once they saw Moira, they flew over to her sobbing. Moira stared at the pixies, wide-eyed, skin paler than I'd ever seen.

"Anna," I said, guiding Moira to sit in the nearby chair. "The king has been murdered by Stephani, but a guard saw me. They think I killed the king and will be searching for me."

Anna glanced at Moira then back at me. "So tell them you didn't!"

Squaring my shoulders, I stood straighter. "Words may not be enough."

"No," Moira reached for my hand, and I gave it to her. "I will not let them hurt you. Tallis, I need to finish this."

Without her explaining, I knew exactly what she meant. "Where's the crystal dagger?"

Moira slipped a hand into her left pocket then the right. "I . . . I don't have it."

"It must be back in the room. Stay here."

Leaning down, I kissed her on the top of the head. "Tend to the wound on the queen's wrist and shoulder. I'll be back soon."

I raced down the secret passageway that would lead me back to the king's chambers. Using my wind ability, I moved quicker than normal. Slowly, I opened the passageway. Kyros' eyes were closed, and he was slumped over on the floor. Kane kneeled on the ground, crying over him.

The door to the bedchamber was closed, no guards in sight.

I walked in. "Where are the guards?"

Kane looked up at me, his shoulders shaking. "I sent them away. Who did this? Who killed my father? Was it the same one that killed my sisters?"

"The witches. They had planned to eliminate everyone and take the queen's place."

His gaze moved to Stephani who laid on the floor. "I never liked them. Were you here when it happened?"

I shook my head.

"My mother was covered in blood. . . so are you." Kane pushed aside the front of his father's tunic, his brow narrowing before his gaze landed on something on the floor. He reached over and picked up the queen's moonblade. "This is my mother's."

"It's not what you think. A lot has happened in your absence."

He stood; black shadows wafted off his skin. Before we had sent him to the dryads, his elemental ability had not manifested, and now it did. "The wound in my father's chest . . . that's not from a normal blade."

"Shadow magic," I whispered, surprised he received that elemental power when it hadn't been seen in the fae for generations.

"Yes, one of many things that happened during all the years my mother abandoned me."

"It was days here."

"I don't care! She should never have sent me away. And this is what I come back to? My father dead. Was this her plan the whole time? Kill my father without me around to stop her?"

By the bed, near the floor, lay the jeweled dagger. I'd need to move quick.

"She killed him." Kane's shoulders shook. "I knew she was jealous of the witches, but this . . . how could she? She will answer for her crimes. You both will."

With a flick of my wrist, I swirled the air around the dagger, lifting it off the floor and sending it flying at Kane. It sliced his arm and was in my hands before Kane could register the attack. "Be a righteous king and don't believe the lies that you're about to hear. Everything your mother has done has been to protect you."

Kane screamed and shot a stream of shadows at me. I twisted away, swirling back through the passageway.

His scream echoed behind me, and footsteps pounded against the stone corridor. I flew into the queen's chambers, and before she had time to ask, I grabbed her by the waist and soared out the open window.

"What are you doing?" Moira yelled, grasping at my chest.

"Moira!" Anna screamed and slammed into the magical barrier, trying to follow us. Ella banged on the invisible wall, tears streaming down her face.

"Tallis, stop! Go back!"

"There's no time. Do you have the stone from the lich?" If she did, we could at least finish the rest of this disastrous mission.

"Yes, but why are we leaving?"

A roar sounded in the distance, and I glanced behind us to see a black dragon chasing after us through the sky.

"Is that Kane?" Her voice dropped and she squeezed me tighter.

"Yes, and he's gaining ground. Do you still have that transporter rod." I flew closer to the mountain floor, zipping through the trees.

The dragon flapped above us, spewing a black breath weapon.

Gripping my neck, she nodded.

"Picture somewhere safe and let's go. I'm going to fly us through that thick wood where it'll be harder for him to get to us."

She took the transporter rod out of her cloak.

Trees flew past. Twisting my body, I maneuvered us closer to the ground and around the forest.

"Now," I yelled.

A portal appeared in the air, filled with green leaves and bright flowers. We flew in. As soon as we landed, I swung around. Moira's son, now a dragon, swooped down toward the portal.

He'd always had his father's eyes. And now they were filled with rage.

CHAPTER SEVENTEEN
MOIRA

Pressing the activator rune, the portal closed just as Kane breached the distance, almost making it through, his massive maw snapping at us.

I stood there staring at the last place I saw my son.

How could so much have happened in such a short amount of time?

"Where are we?" Tallis asked, speaking quietly, his hand on my waist.

"Nightsong Jungle. We should be safe for a while." I turned to him. "What happened?"

Taking both my hands, he held them tightly.

"He believes you killed the king. He found the moonblade. There's no knowing what he'll do."

Ripping my hands out of Tallis' grasp, I covered my face, falling to my knees.

Kane . . . I can't leave you.

"I should go back," I said, staring at the blood still on my clothes. "I'll explain everything. I'm still the queen."

Tallis kneeled on the ground. "Not now. He won't listen to reason, and I don't want you to get hurt. What about this?" Tallis slid the dagger over to me. "Kane's blood is on it."

"You hurt him?"

"Just a deep scratch, enough to capture his blood like you needed."

I took the phylactery out of my pocket and held it over to Tallis.

"Are you sure you want to make him immortal?"

"There is still one witch alive," I said softly,

my heart conflicted, but my mind forcing me to make this decision. "I'm not there to protect him, but with this . . . no one will hurt one of my children again."

Tallis took the blade, slick with the blood of my son and his father, and flattened it against the stone, dragging it across on both sides until the green shiny surface turned deep red. I took that stone and lifted it to my mouth and recited the words the Lich King had given me. With each spoken word, the stone hummed, warming in my hands. The blood seeped inside the stone, swirling inside the center, changing the plain green stone into a glittering jewel. It glowed, the red swirling inside like a hurricane.

"Is he immortal now?" Tallis asked.

Other than blind faith in the promise of the Lich King, we had no way of knowing. "I hope so."

"What do we do with the stone? We can't walk around with it. We should bury it somewhere safe. Any ideas?"

I looked around at the area, searching for anything familiar, but we were outside of the fairy village, far from anything that I knew. "I don't know. This stone is bound to Kane's soul. It must be protected."

Tallis reached over, took my hand, and lifted me to my feet. "There's a stream over there. Let's wash you up."

Slipping the stone into my pocket, I held his hand and walked over to the grass, finding a soft patch to sit on.

Sunlight beamed in through the branches that created a canopy around us. Whistling birds sang in the afternoon. I sat, feeling empty and lost. Tallis made a cup of water with his hands, brought it over to mine and rinsed the blood off my hands then my arms. Then he gently tugged me closer to the water dipping my fingernails in until none of the red was left.

"We're going to be okay," he said, wiping my face.

Though, I wasn't sure we were. My daughters were gone. The king was dead. My son alone, immortal, afraid, angry and I wasn't there to ease any of those pains. I had failed all my children and now I was to roam the lands in exile while my son hunted me down to slaughter me like cattle.

I was so tired. So exhausted.

With a gentle touch, Tallis used his fingers to remove the remnants of today off my cheeks. "Let me see your shoulder."

Ella had done her best to dress the wound quickly, but blood had already seeped through. Slipping the strap down, I examined the cloth tied around my shoulder.

"We should re-dress that now." Tallis removed his armor and then his tunic, ripping a long piece off.

The air had a sweet floral scent, dewy like afternoon rain. The stream moved lazily and across the water, I spotted two big bullfrogs sunning themselves on rocks.

Something pressed on my shoulder, and I cried out.

"I'm sorry." Tallis leaned over and kissed my cheek. "I should have never left your side."

Closing my eyes, I breathed in his airy scent, unable to respond. Words seemed useless. Every choice I'd made led me to this moment and though I was separated from my son, I didn't regret any of it.

They all deserved death for attacking my family.

Every.

Single.

One of them.

"There." Tallis wrapped the cloth around my shoulder. "Your wrist isn't bleeding as much, but we'll need to make sure the cut doesn't get infected. Who bit you?"

"Stephani," I croaked. "Ella applied one of her tonics incase the witch had tried infecting me with something."

Though I could feel Tallis holding me, everything went numb, the questions and worry disappearing until all thoughts left my mind.

I didn't ask where we were going or what would happen next. Did it even matter?

Holding me in his arms, we walked through the jungle, Tallis humming a soft tune to ease my pain. Would I be able to return home?

What would happen to my pixies? And Olivia . . . I still didn't know if she would survive. She had to though. I couldn't bear the thought of her passing.

Since Catriona's death, life began spiraling and I didn't know how to stop it. Was this the end or were there more horrors waiting on the horizon?

The land rose and we crested a hill, the jungle opening a bit. He sat down, keeping me in his arms, never once releasing his hold. On the hill we had a perfect view of the life tree where all life in Saol centered around. Massive protector raptors glided around in the sky, keeping predators away. Their green and glorious golden feathers created shimmers across the sky.

The gargantuan tree soared past the clouds, disappearing out of sight. It was the birthplace and the heart of our world. It seemed fitting this was where my current life would end. I'd never be able to see my son, never hold him again, never tell him how much I loved him and explain how everything I did was to protect him.

Now he would be the one to deal with the Lich King and the bargain I made.

Kane wouldn't be the only fae to hate me.

I'd left the kingdom a mess. If only I had acted sooner. Maybe then my daughters would still be alive.

Pain radiated from my temples, a pounding in my head to drown out every thought.

I leaned my head against Tallis' chest, curled in his lap.

He slid his hand around my neck, thumbing my cheek. He kissed the top of my head, holding me as tight as he could. "I may not be able to remove the sorrow, but I will embrace it with you."

I pressed my face against his chest, breathing in his familiar scent. "I've lost my whole family."

"You are not alone," he whispered into my hair. "I've been with you since the day you were born and I'm never leaving."

Knowing words could never respond to something so pure, I leaned up and kissed him softly. A sob erupted from my chest and Tallis pulled back to hold me. He rocked back and forth, stroking my hair and humming until the sun set and the tears stopped flowing.

EPILOGUE

ONE YEAR LATER
MOIRA

Tallis walked into the tent wearing a wide smile. "I found it!"

"Finally," I said. "Hurry and get inside."

I leaned back in the chair, thankful Tallis had adjusted the hinges so this would be more comfortable. He sat in a chair behind me and leaned over.

"You might be more relaxed without this." He plucked at my shirt, and I swatted his hand away.

He laughed and gave me a quick kiss before grabbing the water basin.

"Did you get the right dye this time?"

"Yes, your majesty." He dumped the cold water on my hair, and I squeaked.

"This better not have any leeches," I grumbled, remembering the nightmares I had after the last dye he brought me.

"No bugs, promise. This one is redder though, a mix of berries and evening primrose." He dragged his fingers across my scalp, soaking the strands.

Closing my eyes, I sighed. For someone who never tended as a servant, his hands moved better than any stylist I had ever experienced. This was my favorite part of the month, and I don't think Tallis minded, for throughout the dying process, he would lean over and give me plenty of kisses.

Humming, he worked the dye into my hair, then twisted it all up. "Done."

With Tallis still holding my hair, I slowly rose. He tied the shorter strands into a bun, then secured it with the pins we had purchased from the local merchant. "There. The woman said we need to keep it saturated in the stain for a while. Hungry?"

"Starving." I grabbed the nearby shawl and wrapped it around my shoulders.

Tallis wiped the area near my hairline with a wet cloth. "I got a little on your skin, sorry."

"It's okay."

He leaned over, taking my face within his hands and kissed me. "First, we eat, then we bathe."

With a pat on my backside, he winked and walked out of the tent.

I laughed and followed.

So much had changed since we left the palace,

and though the pain of that week still lingered, I'd found joy and peace in this little village and the life Tallis and I had built together.

He sat at the wooden table in front of our almost finished cottage. We were so close to finishing our home. The thatched roof was completed, the floor and walls painted and sanded, the only thing left was the furniture which the woodcutter said would be finished by the end of the week.

Tallis scooped out fresh bread from a bag and placed it on the table. "The shop next to the baker had this new dish . . . it's a mix of rolled dough into tiny pieces with cheese cooked in the center."

I sat, smiling as he handed me one. "It sounds wonderful."

A fluffy tail rubbed up against my leg. "Hello."

I picked up the red and black fox that had adopted us.

"He's just here for the free food," Tallis grumbled, but then scratched the critter's head. "I have something else for you."

He straddled the wooden bench, facing me, the afternoon breeze blowing his shoulder length hair. Thanks to all the work outside, the sun had bronzed his skin, almost making the golden runes impossible to notice.

Placing the fox back on the grass, I slid forward. "Is it edible?"

"Of course, your majesty."

There were many comforts I missed from home; food had been one of them. I opened my mouth, waiting for whatever delectable treat Tallis had found. He'd done everything to appease me, and I'd never been more grateful.

Sticking his hand into the paper bag, he pulled out a brown square.

Please, tell me that's chocolate.

Gently, he placed the treat in my mouth, and

it melted on my tongue. I rolled my eyes, the exquisite fudge far better than I remembered. Before he could pull out another treat, I grabbed his face and kissed him. He groaned as I slid forward, climbing onto his lap.

His hands slid up my neck and right into my hair.

"Ugh," he pulled back, having forgotten about the dye. His hands had streaks of red and he wiped them off on his pants.

Laughing, I kissed his ear, making him groan again.

"I think it's time for a bath." He scooped me up into his arms. "Hope the lake isn't too cold today."

Smiling, I laughed as he ran.

A portal opened, the glowing circle sliding him to a stop. Quickly, he placed me down and shoved me behind his back. "Go to the tent."

The blurry image cleared, showing a lavish

room and then a dark-haired pixie flew out.

"Olivia!" I ran to my friend.

"Moira!" She flew to my face and squeezed my cheeks. "You've gained weight!"

"That's the first thing you have to say?" I held out my hand and she landed on top of it. "What news do you bring? How is Kane?"

She frowned. "Spoiled as ever. Is that chocolate I smell?"

"Yes, want some?" Tallis draped his arm around my shoulder.

"Of course, I do!" Olivia said, flying up to Tallis and kissing him on the nose. "I hope you've been doing a good job serving her majesty?"

Tallis' eyes sparkled. "On my hands and knees."

Olivia giggled and I nudged his side. "I think I liked it better when you kept your thoughts to yourself."

"I don't," Oliva interjected.

We walked back over to the table where Tallis offered Olivia a piece of fudge and she grabbed the entire bag. I hadn't seen her since the night we left the castle. After a few weeks, I sent a message to the pixies and only one they would understand. It took the pixies months to find the right village, but once they did, we made a promise to see each other, if only for a few moments, at least once a month.

The fox jumped onto the table, sniffing at Olivia.

"Sit!" she said, pointing at the animal.

And he did, and she proceeded to use him as a backrest.

Tallis pulled me onto his lap, shifting me so he didn't rub up against my wet hair.

"How is Kane, *really*?" There were rumors that since Kane had discovered his immortality he'd been . . . difficult to deal with. Even the Magi Council had kept their distance. "Has he married yet?"

"No, he won't even entertain the idea, but the priests keep pressing the issue, saying there must be an heir and rambling on about some prophecy."

"This is my fault. I should have stayed."

"No." Tallis rubbed my back. "We did the right thing."

"Tallis is right." Olivia bit into one of the chocolate squares. "Kane still blames you, though I've explained the truth a million times. He's so stubborn, but he is okay. I mean, no one can kill him. You're better off here."

"He's angry," I said, taking Tallis' hands. "Kane has every right to be."

"I should go." She took another square of fudge.

"But you just got here!" I reached over to her. "Why are you going so soon?"

"Because I have to, and because you need to

wash that gunk out of your hair. I really miss your natural color and why did you cut it?" Olivia flew off the table.

"I like it. Short hair suits the queen well." Tallis kissed my cheek before letting me go after my friend.

"*Please*, stay just for a bit longer," I begged.

"Well, maybe. Kane barely needs me for anything useful." Olivia's gaze dropped to my stomach. "When were you going to tell me about that?"

"About what?" I looked down at my shirt, seeing just a spot of reddish brown near one of the buttons.

She flew over and lifted my shirt.

"Olivia!"

Tallis laughed behind me, and I glared at him. "A little help?"

He shook his head and backed away. "Oh, no, this is a queen maid thing, clearly."

"Ouch! Olivia, your hands are freezing!"

She poked at my belly before flying back up to my face. "And you're with child!"

"What?" Tallis and I said at the same time.

Olivia clapped her hands. "You didn't know? Oh, this is so exciting!"

I turned to Tallis, shaking my head. "I'm too old. I can't be."

His gaze went to my belly. He slid his hand over my lower stomach. "And here you thought the baker's honeybuns were making you gain weight."

"How can you know this?" I asked Olivia, tears in my eyes, hope blossoming in my chest.

Smiling, she flew to my shoulder. "I'm a pixie. We know everything."

I wanted to believe it. I dared to.

"A baby," Reaching out for Tallis, he grasped my hand, keeping his other on my belly. "Our baby."

"I'll give you two a minute." Olivia fluttered off, leaving me and Tallis alone.

"I still don't believe it . . ."

"Believe it," Tallis said, pulling me into his arms. "We have a chance to build a new life, one with no obligations, other than to each other."

I glanced at the cottage, to the flower and vegetable garden we had planted together, and at the home we created with our own hands. We had changed our future, and for a time I thought it was for the worst, but now, I understood we were *exactly* where we were supposed to be.

The end.

THANK YOU FOR READING!

If you'd like to learn more about the world of Saol go check out the completed Fantasy Romance series, *The Shifting Fae.*

This completed series comprises of stand-alone romances within a connected series arc where in book 4 previous couples show up for the final battle against the Rift.

https://elizatilton.com/books/series/the-shifting-fae/

About the Author

USA Today Bestselling author Eliza Tilton graduated from Dowling College with a BA in Visual Communications. When she's not arguing with excel at her day job, chasing after four kids, or playing video games, she's writing Timeless Romance & Epic Fantasy. Check out www.elizatilton.com for more of her books or follow her on tiktok @elizatilton where she shares tons of bookish stuff.